A Sock Full Of Holes

Jacob Snodgrass

Table of Contents

Thank you to everyone who helped and inspired me:

Sondra, Joe, Gretch, Mom, Dad, Rob and Dave.

I'm lucky to have you.

Like It Was Something
Good On TV

When I was living with my sister, we got into the routine of going to the Elks every Wednesday for their fish fry, and after awhile we got to know one of the bartenders there, a guy named Vince. He was pale and thin, about forty years old, with wispy blonde hair and a dead tooth. He had an ugly, skeletal face, but his voice was deep and appealing, like that of a county-western singer.

One time, after we had been going there for about six weeks, Vince came over and asked us for our orders, but instead of the usual—fish, slaw, and a Crown & Coke—my sister said, "Vince, all I want is a kiss." But Vince just flashed her his dead tooth and walked away.

Later that night, after we'd had our fill of fish and were deep into the drinks, Vince came back and hung out with us. After awhile, he picked up my pack of Winstons and lit one for himself without even asking, but I didn't really mind because Vince always treated me good when it came to the drinks. And then even later, he pulled my sister over onto his lap and started whispering in her ear. And then he started kissing her with long silent kisses—and I just sat there, drunk, watching them like it was something good on TV.

*   *   *

One morning, my sister and I were sitting on the couch, watching

The Price Is Right, when my sister pulled out a state ID that she had gotten the day before.

"Don't I look like Aileen Wuornos?" she said as she handed me the ID. "I told the lady at the DMV that when I show my ID at the bank, the teller is going to say, 'Well, hello, Aileen, we thought they killed you!'"

I looked over the photo and then handed it back to her. "It isn't a perfect resemblance, but—"

"I look so hardened!"

"Yeah, but you don't really look like—"

"I look like Ma Barker, that's what I look like!"

"Yeah, or maybe Aileen's sister, but not so much like Aileen herself."

"I need a face lift bad! Do you know any plastic surgeons, or anyone who has gone to a good one? I need a really good one!"

I lit up a cigarette and rested it in an ashtray on my knee. "Do you want one that can make you look more or less like Aileen Wuornos?"

"Less! Less! I can look more like her on my own!"

We both laughed, and then my sister grabbed the remote. "I can't stand this commercial," she said and started to furiously flip through the channels.

I went into the kitchen and came back with two beers and a whiskey. As I sat down, I gave my sister a beer, and then took a sip of my whiskey followed by a slug of beer.

"What's the name of that schizophreniac you used to take care of when we were growing up?" I asked.

"Which one?" my sister scoffed.

"The one who lived down the street from us. The one who communicated with Hamilton, Ohio, by talking to the ceiling."

"Eva Mae."

"Did she talk to Hamilton every day?"

"Oh, yeah, all the time! And if Hamilton wasn't talking back, she'd put her underwear on her head and get into bed and completely cover herself up with a sheet and lay there as straight as a board and not answer to anyone. And the only way we could coax her out was with her sweet milk."

"Sweet milk?"

"Yeah, that's what she called her vitamin drink. It was the only thing she'd eat! She was super skinny...I mean, like ninety pounds! And her teeth were thin and as black as a rat's."

I took a drink of my beer and looked at the TV where my sister had turned it back to *The Price*. I wanted to ask more about Eva Mae, but my sister hushed me and pointed at the TV where the Showcase Showdown was about to get underway.

*   *   *

Later that morning, Vince stopped by with some beer. He and I started drinking, while my sister went in the kitchen and cooked us some sausage and eggs.

After awhile, Vince slid a cigarette from my pack and lit it up. With the cigarette bouncing between his lips, he said, "What movie do you think has been seen by the most people? *The Wizard of Oz*? *Star Wars*? *Titanic*?"

I stared at the TV where an episode of *The Golden Girls* was muted. "Who cares," I said.

"Come on, have a guess."

"I don't think so."

"Come on."

My sister stuck her head out over the bar. "*E.T.!*" she yelled. "*E.T.!*"

I rubbed my forehead with my hand and continued to stare at the TV.

"Come on," Vince said.

I dropped my hand into my lap. "All right," I said, "*Logan's Run.*"

Vince wrinkled up his forehead. "That futuristic flick? Come on, man, that didn't even show in theaters."

"I don't give a fuck if it didn't show in the theaters," I said as I reached out and slid my pack of cigarettes towards me. "It's still my guess."

Vince shook his head and blew smoke out of his nose. "Yeah, well, I sure as hell ain't never seen it."

"Whatever."

"Not from beginning to end, I haven't."

"Whatever."

"I haven't."

"Whatever."

Vince crushed his half-smoked cigarette into the ashtray, and started to get up, but my sister came around the bar, carrying two plates of food for me and Vince.

"Well, what was it?" she said. "*E.T.*?"

"Aw, who gives a fuck," Vince said as he took his plate and sat down. Then after taking a bite of his sausage, he said, "This is freezing cold." He dropped his fork onto his plate and shoved it away. "How is that even possible? Huh?"

*   *   *

My sister and Vince fought a lot, but that was to be expected, because my sister has fought with every man she has ever known for more than twenty-four hours. But one night they had a huge blow out—one that was more fucked up than usual—and I could tell that it was over for good.

After the fight, Vince went out to his car, and my sister went in the bedroom and cried. I went outside to tell Vince to stay the fuck away for good, but somehow I ended up taking a ride with him and picking up some beer.

"I'm sick to death of these bitches," he said as he aimlessly steered us through town. "I don't need any of them. Right now, I've got three chicks that I'm fucking on a regular basis, and there could easily be five others—maybe even ten others—that I could get back on the team at a moment's notice."

It was cold out that night, and it must have been late November or early December, because the main street in town was decorated for Christmas. Hanging from every street lamp, I saw candy canes made from tinsel and sparkly lights; and in front of the library, I saw a manger scene with illuminated plastic figurines resting on a bed of hay.

Vince pulled into a parking space alongside the street and we sat there, drinking beers and watching the windshield slowly fog up.

"You know what I'd like to do?" Vince said. "I'd like to get me a video camera and hide it outside my house. And then I'd like to call every one of those bitches and tell them to be at my house at a certain time. And I'd tell them all to wear something nice and to bring me a home cooked meal. Then, on the big day, I'd turn on that video camera, and leave the country—go to Mexico or Puerto Rico or something—and then later that night, you could go get the video tape and send it to me. That's exactly what I'd like to do."

Vince laughed and finished off his beer. He then leaned in front of me, opened the glove compartment, and pulled out a flask. He took a swig and passed it to me, and I took a swig too, and then Vince laughed again.

I almost laughed too, because I started thinking about all those women out in front of his house, all dressed up and holding containers of home cooked food. Then I pictured them all deciding to make the best of it by sitting down on his porch and having a little picnic. And then I thought of Vince getting a video tape of it in the mail. Vince in Mexico or wherever, watching his bitches partake in a potluck on his front porch—that was an image that made me smile.

I handed the flask back to Vince and he raised it in a mock toast and then tipped it back for a swig. He then screwed on the cap, stashed it against the crease in the seat, and said, "Cover me," as he suddenly swung open his door. He jumped out of the car and began running toward the manger in front of the library. As soon as he reached it, he plunged his arms into the cradle, yanked at something, struggled for a moment and then yanked even harder. He then charged back toward the car, cradling a plastic baby as if it was real.

"Let's go! Let's go!" he yelled, even though he was the driver, and then he gunned it as he simultaneously swung the door shut.

*   *   *

When I woke up the next morning, I was on the couch, and my sister was in the La-Z-Boy. She was eating ice cream and watching *The Price*.

I think we watched the rest of the show before I said anything. She didn't even provoke me—she hadn't even said a word—but something about the way she was acting got under my skin.

"It's the same thing all over again," I said. "The same things that attract you to a man are the exact same things that you end up hating about him. That's how all women are—they want it both ways. They want to hook up with a real man, but then as soon as they have him, they want to cut off his nuts. Well, you can't have it both ways. And if you keep thinking that you can, then you're stupider than I thought."

I remember my sister looked angry, like she was going to start yelling at me, but then she just said, "I know, I know," and then let out a couple quiet sobs.

"I'm not saying Vince was anything special," I said. "In fact, that's the point: he was exactly the same as every other man, but until you see that, this is just going to happen to you again and again, just like it always has."

After that, we didn't say any more about it. We just watched TV, and then I got us some beers and we drank for most of the day. I remember we watched *The Munsters* and later we watched *Leave It To Beaver*, and I remember we both laughed pretty hard at both shows. Then I think we both went to sleep.

Me and the Meece

1

We were in bed in a bug-infested flophouse in Baltimore, me and the Meece. The Meece was really named Donna, but everyone called her the Meece due to her cheese-eating tendencies. She had found work dancing. I had found work cleaning toilets.

The TV was on mute; an upright strip the color of an earthworm cut Huckleberry Hound in half. I was in my work clothes: a gray jumpsuit, unzipped. On my naked stomach, I rested a glass of whiskey on the rocks among a scattering of Ritz and black hairs. The Meece, her chunky legs wrapped in grubby sheets, had fallen asleep with a hunk of brie clenched in her fist and purple wine stains on her lips. The skin on her arms was like lunchmeat: speckled and with that unnatural sheen. I thought I could smell raw onions and salami rising up from her stubbly pits.

"Meece, you awake?" I said, trying to wake her, but she didn't budge. "Meece?"

I looked at a fork on an egg-stained plate on the nightstand and considered jabbing her with it—jabbing her lunchmeat biceps—but then my tongue ran over the pair of jagged teeth in the front of my mouth, and I remembered the beating she had given me with a plunger a few weeks earlier. That gave me the strength to resist the fork.

"Meece, I don't think this is working," I said to the lump in bed next to me. "Me and you, that is. I mean, think about it—I never sleep; you always sleep. I hate people, including you; and you hate people, including me. The only thing we have in common is drinking."

I lifted my ass off the bed long enough to reach my hand under our mattress and yank out a Bible. "And now I find that behind my back you've been reading the Bible again. You didn't think I knew that, did you? But I do. I found it under the mattress with Cheetos-stained fingerprints on most every page."

I propped the good book open on my belly and flipped through its pages. I recognized some of the chapter titles, but there were a lot I'd never even heard of. I mean, Nehemiah? Joel? Philemon? Who the fuck has ever heard of those? And I wondered how many of the stories I'd know. A few, I supposed. The Christmas and Easter crap and probably a few other things. I mean, I had never set foot in a church in my life, but it's impossible to avoid the stuff; Christianity is everywhere, even in the shit holes I frequent.

I closed the book, and said to the Meece, "I know what's next; you'll start to watch for the signs, and you'll see them everywhere, like when we first met. When you look at a meatball on the end of your fork, you'll see in its lumpy gray meat a sign of the apocalypse. When you stare into a toilet full of puked up wine and Ramen noodles, you'll see a signal of the coming judgment." I put the Bible back under the mattress, and drained my drink. "I thought we had agreed to give up God," I muttered. "At least I thought it was understood."

I kicked at her legs in their cocoon of sheets a couple times, and when that didn't work, I let out a blood-curdling scream. It conjured up an aggressive round of wall pounding from the pervert next door (which is a laugh, giving all the crazyass noise he makes over there), but not even a snore, or a snort, or a fart from the Meece. Then, inspiration struck: I reached over and pressed the squished ball of brie in her fist so close to her face that I could see black hairs from her nose poking into its soft flesh. As I let go, her nose twitched, and her eyes opened and crossed, staring down at the treat in her hand, which she began to gnaw almost immediately.

On my back, staring at the TV, ignoring the pasty sound of her chewing, I said, "Were you awake to watch that episode of *Iron Chef America* that just ended?"

I heard a phlegmy intake of breath before she peeled off another bite. Then, through gummy chewing, I managed to decipher the words, "No, why would I've? Why did you, for that matter?"

"I know, right," I said, "but for some reason I did, and I can't believe what I saw."

"Live turducken?" she said, but through the mush in her mouth I couldn't make heads or tails of it.

"Live tur-what-en?"

Louder than seemed humanly possible, she swallowed, then angrily said, "Tur-duck-en. A live one. Is that what you saw? They're quite rare, you know."

"Oh, you mean the chicken wrapped in a duck wrapped in a turkey thing?"

"Yeah, that."

Without bothering to turn my head, I began to blindly paw at the nightstand in search of cigarettes and a lighter. "Come on, Meece, you know I don't get down with that sort of mixing up of food stuff. I wouldn't have watched that shit for a second. I won't even eat seafood and meat together, because that shit ain't natural. I ain't cool at all with land animals and sea animals getting all mixed up inside."

"Wise decision," she said with a yawn that I could smell.

I found the cigs and lit one up, while the Meece finished her cheese and began to lick residue from between her fingers. Her other hand had begun to flail about near the floor where her wine bottle had last been seen.

"No, listen," I said, "This wasn't just any old episode of *Iron Chef*. It was a really freaky episode in which Bobby Flay was the celebrity chef, but the challenger was Jeffrey Dahmer."

"Jeffrey Dahmer, the cannibal?"

"Exactly. And get this: the secret ingredient was human flesh."

"How convenient."

"I know, right, that's what I thought too. And, of course, Dahmer defeated him easily. I mean, Bobby Flay's no scrub—he's an iron chef for Christ's sake—but Dahmer won in a clean sweep."

She wasn't believing a word of it, and I wasn't even trying very hard to sell it. It was just some stupid thing I often did: in order to fend off boredom and forget the shittiness of it all, I made up stuff, usually for my own amusement, but sometimes not even that.

Obscenely, the Meece slid her lips around the mouth of her wine bottle and threw back her head; I saw no less than four large pieces of lint (or some other such crap) in her rat's nest of hair. I watched her greedy throat ripple as she drank.

She pulled the bottle away from her mouth with a sickening sucking sound and wiped her mouth on her naked shoulder. "I hate to break it to you," she said, "but Dahmer's dead. He's been dead for years."

She tried to hand me the wine bottle, but I turned it down. I could smell bologna rising from the gunk beneath her fingernails. I poured myself another whiskey from the bottle on the nightstand, lay onto my back, and propped the drink on my belly.

"It must've been a re-run then, I guess," I said.

Neither of us could stand the sight of each other for another second.

2

Me and the Meece met in a funeral home that neither of us had any business being in. I had gone in to get warm. She had gone in to make a few bucks. I sat way in the back, sipping a flavorless coffee and trying to be inconspicuous. There were several rows of people—mostly old ones—sitting on wooden chairs in front of me. The scene was a sea of heads: slick bands of hair stretched over bald heads, sitting next to puffs of white hair propped on top of humps of pastel sweaters, or skeletal forms draped in dresses made from used dishrags. The whole place reeked of roses and incontinence. And the worst sight of all was the dead person: from where I sat, I could barely glimpse her in her cost-cutter coffin up front, but I swear she looked like a mummified corpse that had been plucked from a tar pit after thousands of years and was now quietly decomposing under a shitty orange and brown afghan. Up close, however, I'm sure she was fetching.

At the front of the room, a few feet in front of the coffin, there was a pastor mumbling through a eulogy; it was almost like he was talking to himself. And he was as fat as a tick, and his forehead had this amazing shine to it, as if it were made of wax that had been caressed by only the fingers of the finest virgins. Yet, at the same time he sported this outrageously messy beard; I could see several crumbs and bits of lint in it, even from where I sat.

But anyway, I knew there was no way the old ears in front of him could possibly be taking in his mutterings, but they nodded obediently nonetheless while they decayed away in front of him. I remember thinking, it was almost like their heads and shoulders were operated by invisible strings from some unseen rafters above them. Part of me even began to fantasize that it was all a sham; that maybe at the end, someone with giant scissors would come in and cut the strings, and then lift the dead body from the coffin and reveal it to have been a mannequin or an actual mummified bog person.

However, there was one part of the ceremony that was clearly not an illusion. There was one sign of life. This, of course, was the Meece, but to me, at that moment, she was just a nameless woman holding several long-stemmed roses to her chest. Fumbling with the flowers, she squeezed her way through the rows of chairs, stopping at each person to hand them a card. I knew what this was all about; I'd seen this scam plenty of times, but usually in a bar or on the street, not in a funeral home. The scam was that the Meece was pretending to be a deaf-mute, and her card explained her condition and that she was selling roses to make a living. It made it almost impossible to refuse her, unless your heart was a shriveled, lifeless white turd.

So, according to plan, several people were buying roses from her (anything to move her along as quickly as possible), but there were a couple heartless bastards who ignored her entirely (there's always a couple such fuckers in every bunch). But not me; she had my full attention; I was rapt; I found her fascinating from the very first. She was wearing a men's winter coat that was at least two sizes too big for her, and on its lower back were two muddy butt stains where she had either fallen down or sat down without giving a fuck where she sat. I could only see part of her calves sticking out beneath this, but I saw enough to see what I liked: tattered fishnet hose that disappeared into some floppy, mud-caked high-top sneakers.

I definitely liked her style from the jump, but, unfortunately, I didn't care for her face right away. It didn't have much to recommend it, as far as I could see—it was full and round and pale and a little bit dumb. I did, however, like how her shock of black hair was pulled back in a rubberband that caused it to hang from the back of her head like a rotten feather duster. At least there was that. But then I saw her open her mouth to smile, and I was hooked. The whole upper left side of her teeth was missing. Nothing but a rectangle of blackness... puffy, discolored gums...and likely a stench...

I know it's not for everyone (in fact, I know it's not for almost anyone), but show me a girl with bad teeth, and you've got my interest; show me a girl with terrible teeth, and I just might be in love.

I never took my eyes off her after that, and when I could see that she was finishing up with her little scam, I made my way into the hallway, where I found a seat on some little couch that looked like it was from some old painting. I lit up a smoke and waited. When she came out, she went straight for the exit, but I jumped up and stepped in front of her.

"I dig your style," I said.

"Fuck you," she said.

I told her my name and gave her a drag off my cigarette. Then I flashed her a glimpse of a flask I had in my jacket pocket as she handed me back the cig.

Twenty minutes later, after we had fucked in the stall of the men's room, she was sitting on the bathroom floor with a book she had pulled from somewhere inside that massive coat of hers. I was at the sink, looking in the mirror and picking at a pimple on my cheek, and I could see her behind me on the floor with her legs spread and the book opened up near her cooch.

"What're you reading there?" I said, not really caring, but just passing the time.

12

"The Apocrypha," she said.

That certainly wasn't the answer I expected, but I what did I care.

"That's like the stuff they didn't put in the Bible, right?" I said.

"Yeah. Have you read it?"

I had to laugh at that. "Me?" I said. "I've never even read the Bible."

"None of it?"

"Not a word."

"But you know the stories?"

"Oh, I don't know, I suppose. I mean, who doesn't know some of them? Everyone knows the virgin birth, the crucifixion and all that crap."

She didn't say anything to that right away—she really let that one hang in the air for awhile, and I even thought I saw her wince a little, but I didn't have time to consider it, because this pimple was driving me mad. I had been pissing around with it for several seconds, but it was like squeezing a rock, so finally I just dug into it and raked my fingernail across it, and the thing went nuts.

"Shit!" I said.

"What?" the Meece said.

"Nothing, so long as you've got a tourniquet in that bag." The thing was bleeding like crazy, and I was trying to dab at it to stop it, but it was a geyser. In an instant, I had blood on at least four of my fingers. It was like a scene from H.G. Lewis.

The Meece started to get up, but I waved her off and started pressing some wadded up paper towels against it. That seemed to slow the blood, but then I could see in the mirror a loose, wet juice drooling from the pimple and meandering through the stubble on my cheek.

"Any idea what plasma looks like?" I said. "Is it like a loose, wet juice?"

"I don't know. I don't even think I know what plasma is really."

"Yeah, me neither," I said, and chucked the paper towels in the trash and replaced them with another wad. I could see in the mirror that the Meece was starting to go back to her book, so I said, "Why are you reading that for anyway? Is there some evil stuff in it or something?"

"I don't know about evil, but certainly interesting."

"Interesting, huh? Like what?"

"Well, there's this weird book that I'm reading now called The Infant Gospel of Thomas that is all about when Jesus was a kid, and it's got some wild stuff in it. Like he kills some kids in it."

"For real? That sounds like some evil shit to me."

"I guess. But like check this out," she said as she put her finger on the page. "It says at one point Jesus was making some little pools of water on the shore next to a stream, and some other kid messed them up, so Jesus withered him."

"Withered him? Yikes…what the fuck does that even mean?"

"I know, it's powerful, isn't it? I just picture the blood like evaporating inside the kid and his bones turning to dust and his skin sort of sucking inward. I see him falling over like a withered old twig."

Pressing the paper towels hard against my cheek, I turned around and gave her a long look. "Sounds like you do have a pretty good idea of what withers means," I said.

"Yeah, maybe," she said. "And he messes up other people too. Like he blinds people who hate him, and he kills a boy on the spot for running into him."

"Be a bitch to play tag with him."

"Yeah, but later, he's like a superhero who eventually understands that he has to use his powers to help people and not for selfish reasons. Like when a boy falls off a roof, Jesus shouts his name, and that raises the boy back to life. And another boy gets bit by a snake, and Jesus blows on his wound and it is gone, and he destroys the snake."

"It's always the snake's fault, isn't it?"

"They do seem to get a bad rap in the Bible."

I pulled the paper towel away from my cheek and looked at the bloody, juicy mess on it, and then I looked at my cheek in the mirror and saw that the drainage had finally stopped.

"I guess when I think about it," I said, "snakes can kind of be dicks sometimes. I mean, a cobra or boa constrictor can be a real asshole if it wants."

I turned around, and the Meece nodded at me, but she didn't say anything. She was reading again, and I could see she was already deep into it, totally lost in the words.

3

Me and the Meece, we started out in Boston—that's where the funeral home was—and then we eventually drifted down to Baltimore; and I knew we'd eventually have to drift again once the money got thin, but the thing was, it didn't make sense for us to keep drifting together, because we pretty much couldn't stand the sight of one another by then. But you know how it goes—we stayed together for no good reason. Out of habit, I guess, or laziness or stupidity. Take your pick.

It got so that I couldn't hardly stand being in a room with her, so I started spending more and more time next door at the pervert's. And this guy was a piece of work, let me tell you. Most nights, we could hear his S&M videos blaring through our wall. You'd hear everything—chicks getting smacked around and whipped...chicks screaming their heads off...but even more than that, you'd hear the pervert himself screaming. He'd be doing his own scream in a lady's voice like it was his ass that was getting raped over there. I pretty much pissed myself when I first realized it was him that I was hearing.

Yet, this guy was also—get this—some kind of scholar too. Like he used to be a professor or something, until his various addictions claimed him. I mean, he was for real about it. One whole wall of his room was covered with books. I don't remember the titles or nothing, but it was things like Shakespeare and Poe and those guys. Serious shit. And I remember one time I was over there looking through a little stack of videos he had on top of his TV, and in amongst titles like *Anal Slaves 4*, *Around the World in 80 Rapes*, and *Double Amputee Anal Slaves* was a tape with *King Lear* and *Hamlet* on it. Go figure, right? But that's the kind of weirdo he was.

So anyway, one day I was over there having some drinks with him. I was sitting on an overturned wooden box, while the pervert was sitting on his swaybacked bed. He was a balding black guy—not bad looking for his age—but he had this lumpy gut that extended way further down to his groin than it reasonably should have, which I found a little hard to look at. Even if I wouldn't have already known he was a pervert, there was something perverted about that groin-gut that would have told me he was. It was like he had something down there he shouldn't. A perverted half-being down his pants doing stuff to him while you were trying to have a conversation. It could actually make you retch if you gave it too much thought.

But there he was wearing a t-shirt with soup dribbled down the front of it and pit stains the color of earwax. He had a scotch and water in an oily glass balanced on his knee, and he was telling me about a bar he had gone to back in the 80s when he was staying in New York City.

"Back then," he said, "I rarely strayed from the Bowery, see. I was a mess. I mean, a complete fucked-up mess. You think I'm a mess now? Shit, you ain't seen nothin'. Back then, life was just a haze of rotgut, speedballs and dirty bitches. I'm tellin' you, boy. I mean, if I didn't puke up blood or wake to find myself in a puddle of my own piss, it wasn't a good day. Ya know what I mean? But then there was this one night—the night I'm fixin' to tell you about—where I happened to meet that one guy from the Stray Cats...the singer... what's his name? The white boy with the hair?"

"I have no clue," I said. "I think they were all white boys with hair."

"Who gives a fuck if they were all white boys with hair? I'm talkin' about the one, what's-his-name. Come on, you know *Stray Cat Strut*, don't you?" And then he sang a few lines from it and mimed playing an upright bass.

"Sure, but I don't know that guy's name."

"Sure you do, everybody does. Come on, think! He's a white boy with blond hair done up like Elvis."

"How am I supposed to know it? You're the one telling the story and you don't even know it. You're the one who met him."

"I do know it, but I just can't think of it. It's something like Seltzer…like Brian Seltzer. You know, like the fizzy water."

"Okay, let's go with that then."

"But that ain't it."

"I know it ain't, but it's not important what it is. Just tell me what you wanted to tell me about him."

He furrowed his brow and pursed his lips, and then let a big huff out his nostrils. "Well, it's not really about him anyway…"

"Even better," I said. "Then we don't really need to know his name at all."

"I know, but I sure wish I did."

In silence, the pervert stared up at the ceiling like the name of the Stray Cats guy might gradually emerge from the cracks and stains. I gave him a few seconds, and then I said, "Why don't you go ahead and just tell me the story."

Another huff out his nostrils. "All right, but I'm just going to avoid saying his name when I do. I'm just going to call him 'this guy', okay?"

"Sure, whatever."

"Okay, so this guy…you know, the lead singer of the Stray Cats…what's-his-name…Brian Seltzer Water or whatever…he wanted to take me to this exclusive nightclub. You know, some place I could've never gotten into without him. So, I said, yeah, I'm down for whatever. You know, I didn't give a fuck back then. He could have said we were going to the Son of Sam's house, and if I thought I could get fucked up and maybe get up into some pussy, then I was in."

"Right, I hear you."

"Damn right, you do. So, I was expectin' with him being a big old rock star, that this motherfucker'd be takin' me some place real swanky, you know. Some place real exclusive-like. But this place was a piece of shit. I ain't lyin' neither. I mean, check this shit out: on the front door, someone had nailed up a used condom, and it was all shriveled up and brittle, you know, from being exposed to the elements and stuff, and I didn't even know what it was until I reached out and touched it. I thought it was like a shriveled up baby seahorse or somethin'."

"A what? How the fuck could you mistake a condom for a seahorse?"

"Fuck you, I said it was shriveled from the elements, didn't I? And besides, it was dark as a motherfucker down there. This shit hole was like down some alley that would have been pitch black at high noon, let alone whatever godforsaken hour we rolled up to it. But that's the kind of joint this big rock star Brian Sexton took me to. And I get inside there, and the place is just packed, and I'm like, what gives? I mean, I can't figure out what the draw is, because this place ain't shit, but I figure there's got to be somethin'…hoes in cages, bitches licking your asshole, needles full of smack being passed out like candy…somethin'. And I was right, it sure was somethin', but nothin' I would have ever guessed in a million years."

"Why, what was it?"

"I'll tell you what it was. Way the fuck in the back of this place, after I squeezed my way through this massive crowd of people, I saw that these crazy motherfuckers had built a long jump pit. You hear what I'm sayin'? I'm talkin' about a full-size, regulation length long jump pit with sand and everything. These crazy motherfuckers had had it installed just for kicks, you see. So, everyone's gathered around, runnin' and jumpin' and bettin' on each other's jumps. That's fuckin' crazy, right? I mean, they're laughin' their asses off, having the time of their lives, and passin' around money—I mean big money, like wads of hundreds and shit—and they's passin' it like me and you might pass a joint. Like it was nothin'. Like it was notebook paper, not dead presidents. But still, I'm thinkin', all right, this is different, but what's the big deal? And that's when shit got real wild. Because who happens to be in the bar that night? None other than porn star John Holmes, and the dude is whacked out of his head, eatin' Quaaludes by the fistful, and boastin' loudly about how he's going to beat everyone in the long jump! And naturally, people are goin' nuts eggin' him on. And John's wearing nothin' but cowboy boots with black tiger stripes. Buck ass naked otherwise with that big old dick of his just swayin' in the breeze! And so, anyway, after a big build up, he takes off runnin'—all assholes and elbows and looking like he ain't never run a sprint in his life—and he only manages to jump about two feet and falls flat on his face in the pit. Of course, the crowd goes apeshit at that; they're all pointin' and laughin' and gettin' in his face. But John just gets up, dusts himself off and yells, 'Oh yeah? Well at least I'm staying at the Waldorf!" And then he just walks off into the night, wearin' nothin' but those tiger striped boots!"

At that, the pervert slapped his knee and let out a big, long, exaggerated laugh. And I laughed too. I knew the story was probably a lie, or at least a lot of it was, as was often the case with things the pervert told me, but it was still a pretty good one.

The pervert then downed his drink and lay down on his bed. He often did that sort of thing. Sometimes he'd just lie down and go to sleep while I was there and not even tell me he was going to, or he'd just nod off while sitting right in front of me. Sometimes in mid-sentence without any warning. Or another classic move of his was to simply not turn on any lights as it got dark outside, so that gradually the room would get darker and darker, until I couldn't see a foot in front of me. Then he'd just go real quiet, and after awhile I'd hear his snores. Then I'd let myself out.

This time, though, after he'd been lying there awhile, I reached for the scotch bottle, and mumbled that I was going to stick around a bit if he didn't mind. I replenished my drink and took a sip. I didn't know if the pervert had heard me or not—I couldn't tell if he was even awake—but then, after awhile, without even stirring, he said, "You're havin' troubles with your old lady, huh?"

"Something like that," I said.

He was as still as a corpse, and I couldn't even see his lips part, but he said, "You know what you need?"

"What's that?"

"Shakespeare," he said. "All of life's answers are in there." He didn't exactly lift his arm, but he did point with one finger up at his books. "Get that big book down for me, will ya."

I didn't want to, but I went over and got it anyway, and in the process I made an interesting discovery. Looking back on it, one I wish I'd never made. As I slid the book out, an envelope that had been behind it and a few other books fell to the side a little, and I could see there was money inside it. Quite a bit of money, it looked like, but it was hard to tell how much. And I didn't dwell on it—I didn't want the pervert to know I saw it—so I just went back to my seat with the book.

"You ever read any Shakespeare?" the pervert said.

"No, I only read stuff that's in English." I gave a little laugh, trying to be funny, but the pervert didn't laugh at all.

"It is English, fool."

"Yeah, but it's like Old English, isn't it?"

"It's early modern English, actually, and it's worth the effort."

I held up my glass and studied the oily sheen on the surface of the liquor and the smudges of fingerprints on the glass itself. "Thanks," I said, "I'm sure it is, but I can get my wisdom elsewhere. I mean, it ain't like nothing Shakespeare said hasn't been said better since."

"Said better by who?"

"Other writers, that's who." I took a healthy gulp of scotch and wiped my mouth on my sleeve.

"So, by that logic then, if it's new, it's better?"

"No, not necessarily, because I'm sure a lot of new stuff sucks. I don't know who I am to say that because I haven't read a book in about a decade, but I'm sure the best living writers can capture what was great about the old ones, but without being so boring about it."

"Well, I'm not sure I agree with you there, but for the sake of argument let's just say that's true. So, then, if that keeps happenin', and we keep ignorin' the original source, then don't we run the risk of it evolvin' into something else altogether and losin' the essence of the original? You see what I mean? So, that's why me must continually revisit the classics."

"We? I don't think so. Writers and scholars, maybe. But a bum like me? Probably not so much."

He let out a long, slow breath. "Well, listen, all I'm really sayin' here is that it's goin' to help you, if you give it a try."

I looked at the book on my lap, and then I looked long and hard at the space on the shelf where it had been, and I could still see the edge of the envelope up there.

"I don't know, maybe," I said.

"Trust me, it's goin' to help you with all your problems."

I still couldn't take my eyes off it. "Who knows, you might be right."

I slurped down the rest of my drink, and the pervert became real still and quiet again. It was starting to get dim in the room. Everything was blue, and then awhile later I noticed everything was gray. And then the pervert started to snore.

4

One day it happened, as I knew it eventually would. One way or another it always does. I reported for duty at my toilet cleaning job, and they turned me around and sent me home. Stripped me of my mop and plunger, and said I wasn't fit to clean up the piss and shit of the good folks of Baltimore, because apparently one of my toilet-cleaning brethren had ratted me out for drinking on the job as well as, on the rare occasion, sleeping on a commode in one of the stalls.

So, now I had to break the bad news to the Meece. It had been weeks since we had exchanged a significant word. Between us, it had been nothing but monotones and monosyllables. Grunts, murmurs, burps and farts. And occasionally, if I was feeling particularly chatty, I might break the silence by telling her some elaborate lie, like the one about Jeffrey Dahmer on *Iron Chef*, just to see if she was stupid enough to buy it.

Around 2:30 a.m. I showed up at the place where she danced, a dumpy little strip club called Heathers. From the outside, it looked like someone's garage; inside it looked like a 70s disco that was tacky even then. The walls were lined with warped mirrors that had brown and black discoloration in their corners. Reflected in them, I could see cheap, white Christmas lights dangling haphazardly from the ceiling and garish red, blue and yellow lights intersecting on the empty stage to create a single nausea-inducing color where they met. The place was shutting down when I got there, and a few drunk, loud-mouthed stragglers were still being swept out. The Meece was already at the bar, having a beer and a whiskey. She had a newspaper opened in front of her and a Bible opened on top of that.

"Nothing but lies," I said as I sat down next to her.

She jumped a little, surprised to see me, but composed herself quickly. "Which one?" she said, putting one hand on the paper and one on the book.

"Both, in my opinion."

I gestured to the bartender to set me up with the same thing as the Meece. They knew me there and usually gave me drinks on the house. I used to meet the Meece for drinks there all the time when she first got the job, but it had been weeks since I'd last stopped in.

"Not mine," she said quietly, looking down at the good book.

"Don't I know it."

Earlier that evening, after I had been fired, I went back to our apartment, and as soon as I crossed the threshold, I was smothered by an ungodly stench. It was a stench that I recognized, because it had been building up in the apartment for a few days, but now it had taken on epic proportions. It was a rotten, sour smell that seemed to cling to me and lodge itself in my throat and nostrils before I even had the chance to close them. But as is often the case with strong smells, it was hard to pinpoint its source, because although it was powerful, it also seemed to be coming from everywhere at once. But I did eventually find the evil little fucker: it was coming from a battered shoebox that was hidden in a rat's nest of the Meece's dirty clothes in the closet.

Holding my breath, I kept my face back as far as possible as I lifted the lid. I don't know what I expected to find…severed, gangrenous feet, maybe…or perhaps a dead rat slathered in rancid mayo…but not this. Not five disgustingly moldy blocks of cheese that had been carefully chewed down into the shape of crosses. And beneath them, stacks of newspaper clippings. I dumped the whole mess on the floor, and looked through the clippings. They were about some crazy shit: rapes, kidnappings, earthquakes, the Ebola virus, crap about the Middle East, embezzlements, con schemes, AIDs and just all sorts of murder and mayhem. I knew then and there that she had run back into the arms of her old illness. Not only had she gone back to reading the Bible, which I had broken her of shortly after our first hook up, but her mind had melted down into an apocalyptic cheese soup filled with chunks of evil signs and omens.

The bartender brought me my drinks, and I took a hit off each. In the mirrors before me, I could see the dim outlines of the Meece's co-workers scurrying about in various states of undress behind me. "I've got good news and bad news," I said to the Meece as I stared into the mirrors. "Which do you want first?"

"That's what people always say when they've only got bad news," she said. She wasn't looking at me; she was looking at the Bible. She had a coat draped over her naked shoulders, and beneath it she wore what amounted to a sequined brasserie.

"You got me there," I said. "So, you ready for the bad?"

"Sure, why not."

"Yeah, why not. Fuck it, right?"

"Yeah, it's not like you can't tell me anything worse than what I already know."

"Because of the apocalypse, right?" I said, and she tried not to react—she just kept boring holes through her Bible—but I could see that I had caught her by surprise. "Well, listen here, Meece, I might as well tell you that I found your little box of cheddar cheese crosses and wacko newspaper clippings. It's some pretty effed up stuff, really, if you ask me."

"Munster."

"I'm sorry, what?"

"It's Munster cheese, not cheddar."

"Oh, well, you're going to have to fucking forgive me there; the green hairs and lichens tended to obscure it somewhat."

"And besides, that's my private property."

"You mean, it was your private property, but once its stench took on a life of its own, it became a public fucking problem. Besides, I knew you were back on the Bible anyway."

"Good. And I knew you knew, so we're even."

The Meece finally looked at me, and I gave her a forced smile and raised my glass in a mock toast, but she just stared blankly, and for the first time I noticed the purple shadows in the pale white skin beneath her eyes.

I took a drink and set my glass back down. "Let's face facts, Meece," I said. "Bible or not, we're doomed."

"I know we are," she said as she looked away and patted her hand lightly on the Bible.

"I meant me and you," I said as I touched her hand to still it, "not all of humanity."

"Oh. That too."

I leaned in close, and she turned her head away slightly, looking down at the book. Gently, I touched her chin with a finger and turned her face toward me. "Listen, Meece, can you give me a second of reality here?" She pulled back a little from my finger but closed the Bible and looked at me. "I got fired from my job today." I said. "Which sucks, right, but it's not exactly a surprise, is it?"

"I suppose not."

"No, it's not, because being lazy and a drunk are never a good combo for keeping a job. Never have been, and never will be. But the real pisser of it all is this: we ain't going to make it for long in this town on one income, so either I need to skate out of here all by my lonesome, or you need to skate out with me real soon, because there's no way we're going to be able to pay for the shit we owe as it is."

"But what about my job? I make good money"

I tried not to be too mean about it, but I let my eyes look around the depressing dump we were in. "I won't even ask how much you made tonight."

The Meece didn't like that comment at all. Her eyes flashed at me and then she squinted real hard. Then she started to franticly yank wadded up bills and a few stray coins from her coat pockets and pile them up on the bar. "There! There!" she kept saying, but in the end there couldn't have been more than twenty bucks total. The Meece looked at it, and then hid her face in her hands and sobbed.

I put my arm around her—probably the first nice thing I'd done for her in a month—and pulled her close to me, feeling her body shake and listening to the wet, phlegmy sounds she was making.

When she finally quieted down, I leaned in close to her and whispered, "What do you think we should do, huh, Meece?"

She didn't miss a beat. "I'm going with you," she said. She stared right at me and started rubbing tears away with the heels of her hands. "I'm going," she said again.

"Why?"

She was staring at me harder than she had been staring at that Bible. "Because I don't want to die alone."

I shook my head and pulled her close to me. She laid her head against my chest. And after a long time of just sitting there like that, she quietly said, "Tell me the good news anyway, even if it's a lie."

I shrugged and gave a mirthless grin that she couldn't see. "Jesus loves you?" I said.

5

There are certain points in time that we can all look back on and say that's when it all changed. That's when it all went down the shitter. And for me and the Meece, this was one of those points, and it was a particularly bad one. The worst, really, because from then on, nothing ever went right again.

My instincts had told me to flee. Flee alone, they said. But the Meece—even if she couldn't stand me anymore, and I couldn't stand her—seemed to need me then like no one else had ever needed me before, and that's a powerful thing. So powerful that it clouds your thinking. Sometimes for months, even years. Sometimes a whole lifetime.

So, on the walk home from the strip club, we hatched a plan. Our arms around each other's waists, we staggered though tiny gray snowflakes as they twirled down from a starless black sky above. Every word we uttered came out with puffs of steam from our breath, and at times I could hear the Meece's teeth lightly chattering and I could feel her shivering against my arm. I told her about the money I had seen at the pervert's but said it was impossible to get at since he never left the place. But the Meece was resourceful, if anything; she came up with a plan that seemed like a good one, although not without risk. Her idea was that we would prey on the pervert's desires; we would lure him over to our place with the prospect of a little S&M fuck-fest with the Meece, which he wouldn't find odd at all since he knew she and I were on the outs. I'd slip out of the room to give them privacy, and then once I had broken into his room and gotten the money, and the Meece had him securely tied up (which he would be more than willing to allow her to do), I would come back for her and we'd make our escape. It sounded almost too good to be true when I thought about it.

As expected, it turned out to be as easy as I had hoped to lure the pervert into our trap. The next time I visited him, I played up my lady troubles and explained that even in the best of times she had certain wants and needs that I wasn't into, but which I knew the old pervert was. I told him that now that our relationship had been in the deep freeze for so long, she was starting to get like a cat in heat and was driving me crazy with it. So, I wondered if he and I couldn't do each other a favor, seeing as how his perversions leaned the same way as hers. Man, you should have seen the pervert drool over that. He tried to play it cool, acting relaxed about it all, but if I would have given him the go ahead, he would have torn his clothes off and run through the wall to get at her then and there. Instead, I told him we'd set it up for the next night, about 8:00. And I told him to bring a bottle of scotch, too—something good, not the cheap shit—figuring I probably could have told him to bring the Statue of Liberty, and he'd have found a way to rip it up and lug it over rather than run the risk of missing out on this rare chance to get freaky with a real live girl.

So, the big night came, and you can bet the pervert was there at 8:00 sharp, carrying a fresh bottle of good scotch. He was looking pretty dapper too, at least by the pervert's standards. He was wearing the same janitor's pants that he normally wore, but his t-shirt was virtually stainless and he appeared to have put something in his hair to give it a little sheen. He had some sort of smell going on too; I assume it was supposed to be a good one, but it came off more like a mixture of Clorox and glazed doughnuts.

I was the one who let him in, but he practically walked through me like I was a ghost as he made his way around to sit next to the Meece on the bed. She was all dolled up for the occasion, at least by the Meece's standards. She had some tattered fishnets on, a black pleather skirt, her stripper bra resting atop her fat white belly, and a lacquer of baby blue eye shadow on each eyelid.

We didn't have any chairs, so we all three made cozy on the bed. I got some greasy glasses and a bucket of ice, and the pervert, smiling at and eyeing up the Meece the whole time, splashed us out some drinks. After a while, I put one of our three records on the hi-fi and turned the lights down low. When I made it back to the bed, the pervert was already rubbing on the Meece's chunky legs and making an awkward sort of effort to lay his head against her tits.

After I had another drink, I told them I had to run out for a few things, which the pervert knew in advance would be my signal for him to get his freak on. So, I got my coat and headed for the door, taking one last look at the two lovers before I left, as well as our bags, containing all of our essentials, which were packed and waiting under the bed for our escape.

When I got out into the hall, I waited a long time, holding my breath and listening. I could still hear the record crackling away on the hi-fi, and occasionally I heard the Meece or the pervert say something, but I couldn't make out what it was. It was just a muffled high voice and a muffled low voice. But after I had waited a long time and heard their muffled laughter several times, I felt confident that the pervert wasn't going anywhere. So, I made my way over to his door and turned the knob slowly. I didn't expect it to budge. I figured he would have locked it and thought I might even have to break in, but the knob turned without a squeak and the door opened without a sound. But that would be the last thing that went according to plan.

To my complete shock, I found, in the middle of the pervert's room, a big, dark-skinned black woman with a big bottle of wine clenched under her slab of an arm. She had a long, tangled weave that was draped over her head like some old macramé, and she had one lazy eye that sort of rolled around up near her eyelid, but her other eye was piercing and it fixed on me in an instant.

"Who the fuck is you?" she said, and her tone was about hostile they come.

"I'm the…" I started to say, but then I hesitated, because I realized that although I knew the pervert's real name, I couldn't think of it right then, and I couldn't exactly call him the pervert. So, I just said, "I'm the neighbor of the guy who lives here."

"And I'm the sister of the guy who lives here," she said. "And you better have a pretty damn good reason why you's bustin' into his room for."

"I'm not busting into his room. He's right next door in my room. You can go check, really. He just asked me to come over here and get a book we were talking about."

I figured mentioning books might calm her down—let her know that I really knew him, because anyone who knew the pervert knew he liked his books. And when I said it, I glanced over at the shelves to show her I knew all about his collection. And even though I was freaking out and my heart was jumping all around inside my chest, I still had enough awareness to notice in that instant that the Shakespeare book was missing and I could see part of the envelope sticking out. But I didn't dare dwell on it; I looked right back at her, and when I did, to my surprise, her expression had changed. Softened, you might say.

"Well, boy, I'll tell you," she said, "you just about got yourself a show. I was gettin' myself a drink of wine, and then I was about to lay right down here and diddle myself silly. A couple minutes later, and your cracker ass would have walked in on me elbow deep in pussy."

Well, what do you say to that? Nothing. And that's exactly what I said. I just laughed, shook my head and started to slowly walk backwards. At that moment, I would have been all too happy to have just escaped and left the money for another day.

"Aw, hell naw, honey" she said, "you ain't leavin' without havin' a drink with me. If you's my brotha's friend, then you's sho nuff mine too. Besides, you kinda cute for a white boy."

Again, sometimes it is best to just say nothing, which is what I did, except this time I started walking forward as she pulled the bottle out from under her arm and yanked the cork out with her teeth. Then she started looking left and right.

"Glasses?" I said.

She spit the cork out onto the floor. "You read my mind," she said and gave me a big smile. "Glasses, Dixie Cups, sippy cups… whatever you can find. I ain't bourgie."

I gave her a smile back and tried to relax, but I was feeling as jumpy as hell from the scare she had given me. "I think I know where he keeps them," I said, and started to make my way to them, but I never made it. Before I had taken two steps, I heard a sound that stopped me in my tracks.

"My Lord," the woman said, "what the hell was that?"

The sound came again: a frenzied, blood-curdling scream.

"Your brother," I said. "I think."

Then came three screams in a row, the last of which was so crazy sounding that it almost seemed to come from within our room.

"That be him, my baby brotha," the woman said with a big smile and a twinkle in her eye. She held up the bottle of wine and started looking around again, hinting that she was ready for those glasses.

But the screams just went on, over and over, almost without stopping for breath.

"I think we better check this out," I said.

She shrugged. "If you think so."

I ran from the room and had my hand on my door knob in an instant, but I had locked it behind me when I left, so I had to find the key and fuck around with it while that maniac went on screaming, sounding like some sort of howling animal. But I finally got the door open, and there he was, the pervert, laying on the bed spread eagle, completely naked, his hands tied to the headboard and his feet tied to the footboard. His dick was totally and completely erect, and he was throwing his head back, spewing at the mouth and screeching; while the Meece was standing next to the bed, smoking a cigarette, looking down at him with an expression that fell somewhere between boredom, annoyance and disgust.

"I'd slap him if I thought it wouldn't make it worse," she said, but I could barely hear her over his screams.

"Well, someone needs to do something!" I said. "Throw some water on him or something!" And then looking down at his pulsating dick, I added, "Before that thing goes off!"

The Meece actually took me up on my suggestion. She went over to the sink, filled a glass of water, came back and dumped it on him. And that did the trick—his dick instantly went limp and he became completely still and silent.

"Well, that was weird," the Meece said. She took a drag on her cigarette and shrugged.

"Your sister's here," I said to the pervert, and then I looked over my shoulder, expecting to see her behind me, but she wasn't there. "Did you hear me? She's next door at your place."

"Yeah, I heard you" he said in a voice that was hoarse and lifeless. "But I ain't got no sister. Just a brother up in Detroit."

I don't really remember much that happened in the next few seconds after that. Everything just kind of went white. I don't know if the pervert said anything else, and I don't know if the Meece did either. I don't even remember running back over to the pervert's room, or whether his door was open or closed when I got there. I just remember getting there and finding that the woman was gone. And I think I looked at the bookshelf before I noticed the envelope, but maybe not. Maybe I saw the envelope without even looking at the shelf. The empty envelope in the middle of the floor.

The Goon

1

The goon in the next room has taken a strong dislike to me. At one time, we were friends, but now it is as if an insurmountable wall has grown up between us. I offered him a salami sandwich once, as a peace offering, but he refused it. Now, I hardly ever see him; he spends all his time driving around the country in a semi-truck with his new companion, a chimp.

I call this place the monastery, but I'm thinking about changing it to the mortuary. Every evening when I come in, the old Indian woman is pacing the hallway with her head obscured in a veil of blue cigarette smoke. I pass by her room and smell curry and marijuana. I've heard she keeps a raccoon in there; she says it's her dead husband come back from the grave. Two doors down, I see Dwayne wearing gray sweatpants and rubbing himself through them while leaning in his doorway. One starless night, beneath the streetlight out front, he accosted me and begged me to buy his Bible. I refused. I found his desperation distasteful.

In the room between Dwayne's and mine, the goon resides. Through a slightly open door, I glimpse him seated inside. Shirtless and pale, his sternum is pressed hard against his flesh like the breastbone of a baby bird. Perched on the edge of his filthy gray mattress, he combs his long, dirty blond hair by the light of the moon.

It is a well-known fact amongst all of the tenants that the goon hates deaf people, especially deaf children. When he was a kid, the goon rode the bus to school with three deaf kids—two boys and a girl. The boys were much bigger than the goon, and every day, for seven years, they used their size against him; they drug him to the back of the bus and kicked and punched him, and from time to time, let the little girl bite his arms.

One winter evening, after the goon and I had ingested some mushrooms, we stood on the corner, and he rolled up his sleeves to show me. Snowflakes swirled around us, and before my face, blue cigarette smoke twirled. On the other side of the smoke, the jagged tracks of tiny teeth marks encircled the goon's forearms like an unknown alphabet. Fiery sparks began to go off in my mind.

The goon rolled down his sleeves and said, "I watched a movie once called *Sniper's Gonna Git You Sucka.*"

I felt a ball of warm flesh form in my throat.

"It was Boris Karloff's last movie," he said. "The first half of it had a bunch of scenes of him shooting kids on playgrounds. After that, there were lots of scenes of him peeping in windows, watching girls undress. Most of the peeping scenes were shown from his point of view, and you could hear his breathing getting heavy and the camera was jiggling around, so I guess he was getting himself off."

I was listening, but closed my eyes and found that fiery sparks were emblazoned on my eyelids. I saw fireworks, lightning, bombs...

"The only other significant person in the movie was Karloff's friend who was this guy who suffered from agoraphobia. Karloff was always trying to get this guy to go out sniping with him, but the guy always made excuses to get out of it. So, eventually, he gave up on trying to get him to go sniping, and instead got him to go out to the desert with him. They spent the whole night tripping on mescaline and riding around in dune buggies."

In the center of my mind, an alphabet had formed from fiery sparks. I opened my eyes and saw fireworks mingled with snowflakes in the sky.

"That's about it, except the next morning, when Karloff woke up, he said the mescaline experience had changed him. He told his friend that he had decided to never shoot another kid…only adults."

2

Back then, the goon and I used to go on road trips all the time. The last trip we ever took was to New Orleans and then over to Florida. The goon had lucked into some mushrooms, so we ate those on peanut butter sandwiches before we left. Halfway there I started to hallucinate—I saw mysterious paintings hovering over the darkened fields and amorphous fleshy things began to ambulate over the earth.

When we got to New Orleans, we checked into a motel. We spent the next couple hours cutting up porno mags, littering the entire room with a collage of naked bodies. Then I remembered a toy spark gun I'd bought at a gas station, so we turned off the lights and watched sparks until dawn. When I finally closed my eyes, fiery sparks were emblazoned on my eyelids and my dreams were filled with fireworks, lightning, bombs…

Between New Orleans and Florida, at a gas station, I listened while the goon told some truck drivers about how he hated deaf people. Later, at a rest stop, I listened while the goon pedaled his hatred to the maintenance guy. Then, as we entered Florida, he rolled up his sleeves and told *me* the story—the same story I'd heard hundreds of times—but he was telling it like I'd never heard it before. That's when something happened—that's when something came apart inside me.

*   *   *

A couple hours into Florida, we checked into a motel and ingested some acid. The goon cooked up some Ramen noodles, while I read an advertisement for cosmetic dentistry in a magazine. After eating our noodles, the goon and I settled back and watched some Droopy Dog cartoons. We watched until it was dark out, and then I said, "Hey, goon, let's drop a couple more hits and go out," but the goon didn't hear me. He was fast asleep in his chair.

I walked over to the nightstand and opened my wallet. I took out the cellophane cigarette wrapper that held four hits of acid; I slid out two and pinched them between my fingers.

"Goon!" I half-shouted. "Goon!"

He didn't budge.

I held the two hits up before my eyes and examined them. They seemed so small. So, I opened my wallet and took out the other two. "Body of Christ," I said and placed all four on my tongue.

*　　*　　*

I didn't get back until the middle of the night, and then I wasn't alone. I peeked in the window, and there he was, the goon, still asleep by the light of the moon. He and the chair were a purple silhouette, and a shaft of moonlight slanted across his long blond hair.

I signaled for my new companion to open the door while I stayed by the window. My companion passed into the room, becoming a purple silhouette himself, and when he stopped and stood before the goon, parts of their silhouettes merged, so that I couldn't tell where one began and the other ended. I don't know when the goon woke up, or exactly when he saw him, or when the man began to speak to him using only his hands. I just remember hearing a scream, the goon's scream, and I began to laugh; and then I heard my new companion moaning, and the silhouettes began to undergo a violent separation.

When the two men ran out of the room and into the moonlight— one chasing the other—I was no longer laughing. I knew, instantly, that I'd made an irreversible mistake.

I didn't see the goon again that night, and the next morning, when he woke me, I only saw him for a moment. And he wasn't alone. Somehow, in the night, he had procured a companion.

"You've been replaced," he said.

And then he and the chimp, who stood beside him holding his hand, walked out of the room.

What the Sticks Saw

1

Charlie Adams slowly and steadily crushed the doll's face beneath his thumbs, causing viscous red goo to gurgle forth and slither down his hands. Even now, as he looked at the doll, he couldn't completely accept what his uncle had told him.

"I thought there was a niche," Charlie said as he looked up from the doll.

"So did I," his uncle Butch said as he absently passed a doll back and forth between his hands.

"So then what the hell happened?"

"Nothing happened." Uncle Butch fixed Charlie with a stare. "If there is a niche, then it's still there. Somehow, it didn't work. Somehow you didn't fill it."

Charlie allowed the savaged doll to tumble from his hands. "But how is that possible? They're perfect." He picked up another one from the box at his side and stared hard into its papier-mache face.

"I hear you," Uncle Butch said. "You know I thought it'd work too, but for some damn reason the gooks didn't take to them like they did their old ones. It sure as shit don't make no sense to me neither, Charlie. Maybe you just need to tweak them or something."

Charlie nodded and continued to stare at the doll, whose face was painted to look like a young Vietnamese girl. His mind was running in circles. He knew there was a niche in the Vietnamese market, and he knew his product perfectly filled that niche, but somehow every major player in the Vietnamese novelty industry had failed to see this. Yet, here was evidence of his creation's perfection staring back at him. There was nothing about it that needed tweaked. It was simply a matter of the industry either being blind to his talent, or an ignorance of the niche itself, which seemed highly unlikely. No other explanations made sense.

Charlie jammed his thumbs hard into the doll's face, and tiny red candies began to pore out and fall arrhythmically to the floor.

"Red hots," Uncle Butch said with a hint of zeal, but then checked himself, muttering, "Those are rare."

Ignoring his uncle, Charlie let the doll roll off his fingers and plummet to the floor, where a small pile of them had begun to collect. He looked at his thumbs, turning them side-to-side, examining the red stains on them, and he thought of the first time he saw a similar stain on his father's thumbs. It was when Charlie was a boy, and his father had just returned from the war. He told him all kinds of stories about life in the military and the war itself, and Charlie hung on his every word. One of those stories was about a curious type of doll that was especially popular among the cosmopolitan Vietnamese. His father had even managed to bring a few back with him, which he showed to Charlie and demonstrated how they worked. They were wooden and rather large—about the size of an American baby doll—and the craftsmanship on them was shoddy. The dolls were ugly; they were flimsy and obviously thrown together; their hair was glued on haphazardly; and their make-up was garish and crookedly applied. Charlie was even a little frightened by them at first like he facing a voodoo doll or some other malevolent creation.

Each of the dolls came with a small hammer that hung from their necks by either a ribbon or a small length of twine. Charlie's father explained how the Vietnamese tradition was to smash in the doll's face with the hammer, and then eat the sugary red goo inside it with one's thumbs, which he then demonstrated to Charlie's delight. However, after driving his own thumbs into the doll's face and twisting them about before pulling them out with vivid red goo oozing down them, he explained to Charlie that they could not eat it. He explained how these very dolls were some of the last of their kind, because the company who had manufactured them for years was going out of business, because so many people had been poisoned by the goo, which was found to contain lead and dangerous antibiotics.

According to his father, the absence of the dolls was going to leave quite a void in the market, at least for Vietnam's cosmopolitan society. A void that Charlie's father said would someday make a rich man of whoever could fill it.

Throughout his childhood and adolescence, Charlie often thought about the void of which his father had spoken, and when he became an adult he began to work toward filling it. For years, he toiled over prototypes and spent a sizable amount of money on the creation and manufacture of his handmade dolls. Then, six months ago, Uncle Butch took a box of dolls with him on one of his Asian business trips, saying as he left that when he returned it would be with a fat contract that would make the both of them incredibly rich.

"How could they be so ignorant?" Charlie said. "Not only do my dolls fulfill a niche that has been untapped for years, but each one is a unique handmade creation, not some wooden piece of junk crammed together in some sweatshop."

"I know it," his uncle said. "You're preaching to the choir, Charlie."

Charlie lowered his head and stared down at the pile of dolls at his feet. It was like an aerial photograph of a massacre; bodies crosscrossed and spattered with red gore. A plane wreck. Jonestown. Auschwitz. Vietnam.

Within the hour, Uncle Butch was gone—headed for a boat that would sail him to a business deal on the Isle of Wight. In his wake, he left his nephew surrounded by boxes that were stuffed full with thousands of 4-inch tall dolls that were made to look like Vietnamese girls. Before night fell—before Uncle Butch had even set foot on the chalky white hills of his destination—the boxes were stashed away in an attempt to forget them forever. Charlie lugged them from the first floor to the topmost portion of the house and crammed one after another into the deepest corner of the attic, where he intended to house them until the end of his ill-fated days.

2

About two weeks after his uncle left for the Isle of Wight, Charlie Adams began to suffer from acute exhaustion. He would wake up from a full night of sleep and still be tired. He would find himself unable to keep his eyes open, only minutes after getting out of bed. He was even falling asleep at work, sometimes right in the middle of a meeting. In order to get through a work day, he began to resort to regularly ducking into the restroom, where he would sit down in a stall, lean his head against the wall and nod off. There were other unpleasant symptoms as well: sometimes he would perspire profusely, even though he had not been exerting himself in the least; other times his body would be wracked with aches that seemed to gravitate around inside him without rhyme or reason. Like anyone in his condition, he started to frantically visit one doctor after another. Each one seemed as baffled as the one before him, and each diagnosed him differently, treating him for everything from hypertension to chronic fatigue syndrome, but none of their treatments helped in the least. Then, one day, Charlie's pinky finger on his right hand turned black and fell off. A few minutes later, his ring finger also turned black and fell end-over-end to the floor.

In a prickly, stark white, mind-numbing panic, Charlie drove his car at blazing speed in the direction of the nearest emergency room, but on the way, he began to experience excruciating pain in his feet as if vices had been attached to them and were being maliciously cranked shut. While momentarily stopped in traffic, he managed to pry off one of his shoes. At a stop light, he popped the other one loose, but by then the pain had surged up into his legs, causing his calves and legs to rapidly distend. While he idled in the midst of cars and a cacophony of honking horns, Charlie yanked his pants off and chucked them over his shoulder. It was then that the buttons on his shirt began to pop off and ping around the inside of the car like errant gunfire. Mercifully, before he could wrestle with this newest misery, and just after his car ramped off a curb and crumpled against a fire hydrant, Charlie lost consciousness.

When he came to, he was in the recovery room of the I.C.U., lying on a bed, covered in a sheet that was damp with his sweat. His hair was drenched and his body felt like a sponge in a bucket of water. He attempted to lift his head and his arms, but it felt as if an invisible, indomitable force was pressing down on him from above. Without even having actually moved, he collapsed and lay there very still and scared.

"Gwavity," he heard a man lisping excitedly by his side. "The indomitable pull of gwavity!"

Struggling mightily, Charlie managed to inch his head ever so slightly to the side so that he could see the source of the voice. Obviously a doctor, the man was exceptionally short and rotund and wore a lab coat that fit him as snugly as a casing on an overfilled sausage. He had a scandalously sculpted handlebar mustache, and his eyes were non-existent behind his smoky spectacles. Atop one of his foreshortened arms, he shook a meaty red fist at the ceiling in order to emphasize the powerful phenomenon of which he spoke.

"Of courth, Mr. Adams," the doctor resumed lisping at him, "all forms of matter and energy in the erff's sphere, to a lesser or gweater degwee, are drawn toward its center. Without gwavity, Mr. Adams, each of us would be sent hurtling from the thurface of the whirling erff. So, from that perspective, gwavity is, of courth, a good and necessary force of nature. But seen objectively, gwavity, like all of nature, is beyond good and evil. It is a force demonstrable by maffematics, not a whimsical, conscious being. Therefore, this very force that we were so quick to deem benevowent for pweventing us from fwying off into space, can suddenly strike us as mawevowent if we maffematically become too vulnerable to its awe-inspirwing potential."

Charlie blinked twice, and then, in a voice so raspy that it sounded like crumpled parchment, he said "I don't think I've understood a single word you've just said."

"Of courth, of courth, you are in shock," the doctor said, and briefly gave him a hollow smile. Then, he switched his head from side-to-side like a curious animal, before suddenly lurching his whole body forward and spilling out a torrent of words: "Now, the forth of gwavity on an object is called, as you may know, the object's weight. The force depends, of courth, on the object's mass, or the amount of matter in said object. You see, sir, you, Mr. Adams, have become a maffematical disaster. We have determined, fwom our close exthamination of your medical wecords and data that we have collected since your awival here appwoximately 18 hours ago, that within the last 48 hours your weight has gone fwom 210 pounds to 455 pounds to your pwesent weight of 58 pounds. In theory, you should be so light that the force of gwavity upon your fwail being would be gweatly lessened, but in weality, there are other forces at work here, such as air fwiction and, possibly, the perpetuwaytion of unholy corwuption, or even inherited contrition." Dr. Hart paused, took a step back from Charlie and crossed his bloated arms over his belly. "Maybe even the transmigration of a nefarious soul," he said, "but that is quite rare."

It was then that Charlie began to wonder exactly what sort of medicine they had him on, because try as he might to focus, he was having a terrible time making heads or tails of anything he was being told. However, pinned as he was to the bed beneath him, Charlie felt it best to just quietly blink along.

"Perhaps, Charlie, I should begin by discussing your absent little and wing fingers on your wight hand. Now, I want you to pay special attention to what I am about to say, because yours is a particularly rare case. Fortunately, the parwamedics discovered your fingers, which you had wrapped in tissue paper and placed upon your kitchen table. Through varied and extensive examination of those fingers, we have discovered the peculiar essence of your pwesent condition. Let me ask you: your little finger was the first to fall off, was it not?"

Charlie nodded as best he could.

"Wight. About three days ago, I would estimate. Well, bwace yourself, sir, for our tests have unequivocally concluded that your little finger fell off of its own accord. Apparwently, at some point, theveral months ago, your little finger became conscious of itself. Somehow, it evolved a consciousness that was entirely theparate from your own consciousness, and after much fretting over its true essence, meaning and welation to the west of your body and the world around it, your little finger—of its own accord, mind you—chose to enter into a life of extweme asceticism. At first, it wejected all worldly desires. Then, eventually, it wejected all things thuperfluous to maintaining life. And eventually, as you now know, it wejected life itself, becoming, as it believed, one with a thort of divine consciousness."

"And my ring finger?" Charlie managed to interject in a voice that was as dry as desert dust.

"Thame thing," Dr. Hart replied. "sad case, weally. A thort of group phenomenon. Even though it saw the final destiny of your little finger, the wing finger, itself, was alweady too far gone. That is, the wing finger, too, was convinced of a thort of merging with an eternal consciousness beyond the flesh. Of courth, others would have followed had it not been for your thywoid."

"My thywoid?...I mean...thyroid?" Charlie said.

"Of courth! Your thywoid, too, had developed a theparate consciousness. However, it arrived at conclusions that were the very antithesis of those arrived at by your mutinous fingers. Your thywoid, after gweat despair and disillusionment, entered into a life of pure decadence and materialism. This gland du mal of yours, while, on the one hand, intoxicated by a personal thensibility that transcended any weality based on a Hegelian either/or, was, on the other hand, more vulnerable than ever to feelings of existential isolation...feelings that eventually pulled your thywoid down into the abyth. All the while, your body has been a victim to all your thywoid's exthesses and exthemes."

"So, now what happens?" Charlie asked, although he was almost afraid to.

"Well, nothing, actually," Dr Hart said, and then he released a disconcerting titter. "It is gone... totally and completely."

Charlie simply closed his eyes and left them closed.

"That's wight!" he heard Dr. Hart saying. "Glandular suicide via narcithistic gluttony! The thing swallowed itself whole!"

Charlie heard the rustle of the lab coat, as Dr. Hart abruptly turned on his heel and quite nearly marched toward the door. Then, just as Charlie began to retreat once again into the sanctuary of sleep, Dr. Hart came to a halt and whipped back around to face him.

"You understand that they had no other choice, don't you?" Dr. Hart said in measured tones. "They saw what you were doing, and had to turn against you. We humans control almost noffing, and the irony is that the more we try to control things, the less control we actualwy have. Yet, the thing we can control is whether to accept the truth in all its beauty and dreadfulness, or deny it." Then suddenly, Dr. Hart threw his arm up and formed his fleshy hand into a trembling fist, and began to screech and bellow. "But woe unto you who denies it, Mr. Adams! For he is a perpetuwator! He is an abettor of unholy corwuption, Charwie Adams! Do you understand me, sir? Do you yet have ears that can hear, or have you allowed those to atrophy too? Hear this, Mr. Adams, your faithful body had no alternative but to abandon you! It's each man, and pinky, and wing finger, and gland for itself when we have warped weality to such an extent that it is completely and utterly unweal!"

And with that, and a violent lunge, Dr. Hart pushed his way through the door.

Charlie blinked twice. Then he was asleep.

3

Charlie came to with a jolt, but was immediately stilled by a large hand that laid itself over his perspiring forehead. In the dim light of the room, he could just make out a silhouette above him. A tall, gangly man was leaning over him, peering down like a praying mantis over a grasshopper.

Twisting desperately under the man's hand, Charlie tried to raise his head, but he could not even lift it an inch. Even after the man removed his hand, he still could not lift it, as if his head were a bowling ball and his neck a toothpick. Panting and perspiring, he eventually collapsed back into the brown leather couch that supported him, and the man once again laid his hand upon his head.

"Relax, Charlie," the man said. "Your head is simply too heavy right now for you to get up." The man leaned in closer, allowing the fog of shadow to soften around him so that Charlie could see his thick-lensed glasses and crooked auburn toupee.

"Too heavy?" Charlie said as he squeezed his eyes shut and tried to focus his thoughts. "Too heavy with what?"

Gently, the man caressed the moist skin on Charlie's forehead. "Too heavy with dreams, of course," he said.

For some time, Charlie kept his eyes closed, until, little by little, he felt the heaviness depart from his head and settle throughout his various limbs. When he opened his eyes, he saw the man intently contemplating some sticks and even entire tree branches that were scattered over the plush carpet on the other side of the room.

"You were talking in your sleep, Charlie," the man said as he turned to look at him. "Something about dolls in the attic."

"Yes," Charlie said as a wheeze seeped from his constricted throat. "I created some Vietnamese dolls a long time ago, but when they failed to serve their purpose, I packed them away in my attic."

"I see," the man said, and Charlie thought he saw the ghost of a smile cross his lips. "But you know as well as I do, Charlie, that your home does not have an attic."

Charlie opened his mouth, but then closed it. For a moment, he saw in his mind's eye the attic and a memory of himself putting the dolls in it, but then the memory dissipated, and he knew the man was right.

"Do you feel strong enough to recount your dream?" the man said.

After a deep breath and slow exhalation, Charlie said, "I think I can manage that."

Charlie then proceeded to tell the man about his dream, which was essentially the same recurring dream he had experienced countless times throughout his life.

It was the kind of dream that was so startling and vivid that even after he awoke from it, he could not shake the feeling that it was a subconscious recollection of an actual event, rather than a grotesque fabrication. The setting for the dream was always his attic, and there was always an event taking place, such as a party or a rummage sale, and there were always several people in attendance. For the first part of the dream everything was fine; Charlie would be mingling, talking to people and generally enjoying himself. Then, without fail, he would eventually notice something half-buried under some loose floorboards or a rug or a pile of blankets. Upon closer examination, he would discover that the partially buried object was either a jawbone, a row of teeth, a patch of scalp or a collarbone. And instantly, he would be overcome in a rush by both the scent of putrefaction and a vague, yet unequivocal, recollection of his role in the murder and burial of the corpse.

The remainder of the dream was an exercise in anxiety. In every way possible, Charlie would attempt to keep the other people from discovering the corpse, and all the while he would be wracking his brain to try to remember why and how he had come to be involved in the murder and cover-up. Yet, the more he attempted to conceal the corpse, the more it seemed to reveal itself; the stench seemed to fill the air until it entrenched itself in the fibers of people's clothes; and every time Charlie looked at it, more of it was visible: fingernails…a bony finger…a tattered shirt…a crinkled patch of leathery skin…

Fortunately, Charlie always awoke before his crime was discovered. But upon waking, he was always overcome by an oppressive feeling of guilt. He recognized that it had been nothing more than a dream, but he was convinced that the origin of the dream existed somewhere in his past reality.

Throughout Charlie's description of his dream, the man silently listened, holding his hands in front of him with the fingertips of opposing hands softly pressed together. After Charlie finished speaking, the man remained as such for several seconds, then, as if breaking free from a trance, he suddenly swung his attention back around to the sticks and branches.

"As you see," the man said, "I've thrown these makeshift yarrow stalks." He made a sweeping gesture toward the sticks and branches on the floor. "And according to them, you are suffering from one of two things. One possibility is the transmigration of a nefarious soul. However, I find that unlikely, since it is extremely rare. Second, and much more likely, is that you are the victim of inherited contrition."

"And what does that mean?" Charlie said with a croak.

The man leaned in close and whispered, but it was a loud, harsh whisper that was like sandpaper on Charlie's eardrum. "Sin," the man said. "You have inherited sin. But the guilt that comes with that sin, Charlie, that's the true affliction, and that is something you have chosen to suffer from all on your own." The man then peered deeply into the sticks. "The sticks tell me your father was not present when you were born in 1968. Is that correct, Charlie?"

Charlie, bewildered, stared silently into the sticks and nodded. He suddenly felt weightless, almost elated, but when he tried to stand up, the heaviness that had settled in his limbs swelled within him and ascended to his head.

The man resumed speaking, but in Charlie's mind the man's words were buried in a cacophony of gunfire…a fugue of bullets and bayonets in the South Vietnamese hamlet.

Charlie no longer needed the man to interpret for him; he could read the story of the sticks himself. The story of souls colliding at the threshold of being and nothingness…the story of his father, who massacred a village of unarmed civilians, and left in his wake an iniquitous and infinite void.

That Thing Birds Do

1

Mouthpiece of God sounding off behind me. In front of me, raindrops beaded on the window and wood telephone poles black with wet. The haze of pale green, pale blue, pale yellow houses against a sky as white as a corpse. As I turned away, the tang of cat piss stirred under my nostrils. On the carpet, I saw a crumpled beer can and an orange Care Bear with stuffing out its ear.

Perched on the couch, Greg was shirtless. His pudgy arms were crossed over wispy blonde chest hairs and a butterscotch suntan. An old surfer gone to seed. He'll be quite the meal for sharks someday; a bloated brown seal, as far as they're concerned.

Next to Greg was my older sister Maggie. Her mouth was agape and her skin was moist and waxy. Her crooked black bangs were matted to her forehead and reminded me of a raven's broken wing. She was talking at me, but her black saucer eyes never left the TV, and her fingers were outstretched so that she could compare them to what she saw.

"Look at his fingernails," she said. "Did you see them? They're so long and shiny. Davey? Come look at this. This is the guy I've been wanting you to see."

"The televangelist?" I said.

"The one with the sideburns and the fingernails. Wait until you see them. Watch, now they won't show them. Come on, watch. They are so long and shiny, but his fingers are all knobby and crooked like old sticks. Watch, they won't show them now. But you can still see his sideburns. Wait until they show him up close. You can tell he dyes them. They are like jet black with some brown—almost mahogany— mixed in, but he must be what, seventy-five years old? He's at least seventy-five, isn't he, Greg?"

Greg sat as still as a statue, not even mustering a shrug. "Who knows," he said.

"Oh, he's at least seventy-five. At least. Look how loose his skin is. It's hanging from his face. It's just drooping off and swaying there like an old hangdog. That's what he is, an old hangdog. You can even see his skull up there by his temples where it dents in, but look at his lips. Look at them. Like a little angel's. A little apple dumpling angel, all pursed and shiny. I bet he wears lip gloss. He has to. Look at them. Cherry lip gloss."

"Not watermelon?" I joked, and found a seat next to her on the arm of the couch.

She ignored me. "Oh, I wish they would show his hands," she said, "but they won't. Watch, they won't. But you know who this hangdog looks like? Greg knows who, don't you, Greg?"

"No."

"Oh yes you do. Mr. Marshall. Doesn't he look just like Mr. Marshall. Look at him. Really look. Doesn't he?"

Greg exhaled loudly; it was the best he could muster. His pudgy arms unraveled, and in silence he headed toward the kitchen.

"He knows he does. He looks just like him. Mr. Marshall was that guy that lived down the street from us in Florida. I know I've told you about him, Davey."

"The alcoholic insurance salesman?" I said.

"Yes, the one who worked himself to the bone until about one o'clock every day, and then spent the rest of the day in his boxer shorts with his feet soaking in a baby pool in the front yard while he got completely stinking drunk. I mean stinking, stumbling, falling down drunk. But he was a nice man. Always said hi to us when we went past. He was nice, wasn't he, Greg? Greg?"

Leaning in, I whispered, "What's eating him? Seems more menstrual than usual, don't you think?"

"Oh, he's just still mad about me wrecking his car."

"Wrecking his what?"

"His car. I told you I wrecked it when I took it to the laundromat yesterday."

"No, you didn't."

"I did. You don't listen."

"I'd listen to something like that."

"She was drunk!" Greg bellowed from the kitchen.

"Not really," Maggie said as she tilted her head and shrugged.

"She hit a parked car!" Greg bellowed again.

"A parked car? How can you hit a parked car? They don't exactly lay in wait, Maggie."

Maggie shrugged again, and then suddenly shushed me. Her hand frantically patted the couch in search of the remote.

"Wait, turn it up. Turn it up. Wait, watch this. Cagney has bone cancer. You remember I told you about those two, Cagney and Lacey? Well, Cagney had bone cancer, and should have been dead years ago. I mean like eight years ago. But she keeps coming back to this old hangdog for his healing touch. Wait, watch, they'll show his hands up close when he touches her. You've got to see those long shiny fingernails and those crooked sticks. Watch. Watch."

I leaned into her, laughing, and Maggie grabbed my shoulders with both hands, digging in her nails and shaking me as she broke into laughter too at the sight of those pampered hands in close-up. I kept laughing and fell against her; I could feel her moving against me, and I thought she was still laughing, too; but then I realized she had stopped, and it was her frantically waving her hands that I could feel. But it was too late. I turned and saw that Greg had already yanked the wires from the wall and had the TV up over his head. His flabby butterscotch arms were shaking all over, and for a second, I thought it all might come crashing down on his head, but he managed to keep it together and finally let it fly.

When it landed, Maggie covered her ears and squeezed her eyes shut tight, but there wasn't a big crash, hardly even any visible damage—it just landed with a sickening thud, like a garbage bag full of dead cats.

2

I didn't waste any time getting us out of there. Before the dust from the TV had settled, I was shoving Maggie's red leather coat into her arms and dragging her out the door. She was in such a state of shock that I pretty much had to keep dragging her even after we were out, so I put an arm around her and propelled her through the cold drizzle that pecked at our faces. It was early evening, but the streets were dead. Occasionally a car crawled past and water hissed off its tires, but mostly it was just the wet scrape of our shoes as we walked and Maggie's skinny body shivering against me like she had just been fished out of an icy lake. After wandering aimlessly for several blocks, I asked her whether she wanted to go somewhere quiet like my place, or somewhere where we could down some drinks. Maggie gave a shrug. "Anywhere where that asshole's not," she said.

So, we made our way to one of our regular spots, a dive down along the river called Dreamland. Inside the bar, it turned out to be as dead as the streets. No one was sitting at the mismatched chairs and tables scattered around the room, and the little dance floor in the corner was empty. An old Rod Stewart song was crackling out of the jukebox, and off to the side, there were two guys shooting pool and a skanky chick perched up on a stool next to them, but that was it.

Maggie and I took seats at the end of the bar next to the taxidermied turkey that stands with its feet in some sort of hardened goo, and Maggie ordered us a couple beers and whiskies. We'd been coming to Dreamland since before we were out of high school, and we both knew Jerry the bartender like he was family, so I was glad when he started talking with Maggie, because Maggie, no matter what she has been through, has never met a conversation she didn't like. Before I knew it, I could hear her telling him about some advertisement she had seen in the newspaper for a collectable porcelain doll that she swore had his eyes, and while she didn't sound quite like her usual chatty self, she at least didn't sound as messed up as she had on the walk over. That is, until she swiveled around in her seat and slid me my drinks; that's when all the enthusiasm drained out of her voice. "Oh shit," she said, "I can't believe it."

She snapped her head around so that she was staring into the mirror behind the bar, while I looked over my shoulder. In an instant, I saw all I needed to see, and I was kicking myself for not seeing it when we came in—one of the guys at the pool table, who was now chatting up the skanky chick, was one of Maggie's exes, Dennis Garrett.

"Fuck it," I said as I turned around. "Ignore him."

I stared straight ahead into the mirror behind the bar, and Maggie and I tried to drink our beers and whiskies like nothing had happened, but I had a sick feeling in my stomach. There was no way Dennis wasn't going to notice us, if he hadn't already.

Maggie slammed her whiskey, and immediately signaled for Jerry to pour another. "I haven't seen him for years," she said.

"This is actually where you met him, right?" I said.

"Yep. Where else would you meet a rat like him except in a shit hole like this?"

"He was still married then, right?"

"Yep. I don't think he ever wasn't. He probably still is, knowing him."

I gave another glance over my shoulder and saw that the skank had oozed off to somewhere, and Dennis was now leaning against the wall like he thought he was the Marlboro Man. He had on some worn-out jeans and cowboy boots and some sort of Mexican-style shirt. He hadn't really changed much; still a tall, skinny guy with dirty blonde hair. Basically, an uglier version of Tom Petty, and a royal asshole if there ever was one. The kind of guy whose hobbies include hunting, fishing and beating the shit out of his girlfriend. A real piece of work.

I turned back around to say something to Maggie, but to my surprise, I saw three faces in the mirror before us. Standing just behind me and Maggie, like he had been there all along, was Danny Georgiadis, a guy we had known since grade school.

"Where the hell did you come from, Danny?" I said.

"Oh, I've been here all day," Danny said. "I must've been taking a piss when you guys came in, and I was just getting ready to tell your sister here about the bus trip I took out to Vegas last week."

Danny was a barrel-chested guy with a big belly and a rectangular head. He was wearing a black Under Armor shirt and thick gold chain. He had the letters I-C-E tattooed on one hand and M-A-N tattooed on the other.

"The Iceman in Vegas, huh?" I said. "Did you leave anything still standing?"

"Well, I rocked their world once I got there," Danny said. "But getting there was something else." He sat the giant mug of beer he was drinking on the bar top and sort of squeezed his way in between me and Maggie so that he was about an inch from my face. "The bus ride out there was really freakin' weird. I mean, it was like this really nice, luxuriant bus…I mean, like the Taj Mahal of buses, but it was kind of ruined by this guy in the back who kept coughing for the whole trip. I mean, like really coughing, like he had…what's that called, malaria or something? Or whooping cough? Whatever it was, he did it for the whole damn trip. Every ten seconds, cough, cough, cough. So, you can imagine what that was like, and after hours and hours of this, a guy sitting next to me finally lost it and shouted, 'Cut it out!' I mean, at the top of his lungs he shouted it. And you know what? The guy at the back of the bus did. He never coughed again."

"Never again?" I said with a laugh. "Not once again the whole rest of the trip?"

"Not once," Danny said.

The two of us laughed, and I looked at Maggie, expecting to see her laughing too, but then realized she hadn't been listening at all. She was looking across the room.

"Uh oh," Danny said, and raised his eyebrows at me.

I looked over my shoulder and saw that Dennis Garrett had spotted Maggie and was slowly sauntering toward her like he thought he was in a scene from a movie.

When he reached us, he nodded at me and Danny, and then with his legs spread apart like he might straddle Maggie's thigh, he leaned into her and said something in her ear. Whatever it was, it worked, because she laughed, and then she leaned in and said something in his ear. They both laughed, and it went on like that for a couple seconds, before I had seen enough.

Putting a hand to Danny's chest to move him back a little, I leaned across to Maggie and Dennis, and said, "What's going on?"

Dennis gave me a sly smile. "Well, I was just telling your sister here that we're practically neighbors." He was glassy-eyed and I could see every crevice in his long leathery face.

"Oh, yeah?" I said and I could hear my voice start to shake.

"Yeah, I moved out of state for a few years, down to Texas, you know, but now I'm back, and it sounds like I'm about two blocks down from your sis." He gave a little smirk and winked at Maggie. "Maybe y'all could come over for a barbeque or something some time."

I balled my hands into fists. "Yeah, and maybe you could throw my sister through a sliding glass door for old time's sake."

Dennis narrowed his eyes at me, but spoke to Maggie: "Why don't you tell your dad to back off." He sneered and ran his tongue slowly over his lower lip.

I shot up from my barstool and stepped hard at Dennis, and Dennis stepped at me. He was so close that I could smell his macho cologne all mixed up with alcohol and cigarettes, but then I felt Maggie's hand pressed against the middle of my chest.

"It's okay, let it go," she said and held her hand there until I backed off. "We don't need this tonight."

I didn't say another word. I probably couldn't have, even if I had wanted to. At that moment, I was so pissed at both of them that I couldn't even see straight.

Sitting back onto my stool, I stared straight ahead like they weren't even there. A moment later, I heard the scrape of Maggie's stool and saw Dennis and her move away out of the corner of my eye.

"What was that all about?" Danny half-whispered as he settled onto Maggie's stool.

"Nothing," I said. "Fuck them." I took a drink of beer and downed my whiskey. "Tell me some more about your Vegas trip, Danny."

Danny shrugged and gave his neck a couple of quick cracks. "Well, I told you about the bus ride, but that was just the tip of the iceberg. It got weirder when I got there."

"Why, what happened?"

"Well, I was starving when I got there, you know, so I hit The Great Steak Escape they got there by the depot. So, I was standing at the counter, waiting for my food, and there was a guy standing next to me, waiting for his, and I didn't really notice him at first, you know, I was just focused on getting my food. And when my food was ready, they sat my tray on the counter and a french fry fell out of the cup and landed on my tray, and immediately, before I could even lift my tray off the counter top, the guy next to me swooped in like a seagull and snatched up the fry. I looked at him as he popped it into his mouth and swallowed it whole, and he had to have seen that I was shocked, but there was no sign of embarrassment on his face at all. He just said, 'He who hesitates is lost,' and then walked away. I mean, can you believe that?"

"That's crazy," I said.

"Isn't it?"

I sucked down the last of my beer and tossed an ice cube from my whiskey into my mouth. I looked at Danny and was going to see if he wanted to step outside for a smoke, but before I could say anything, Danny said, "I guess nobody puts baby in a corner."

Danny was looking out at the dance floor, and I looked too. Another Rod Stewart song had come on a few seconds earlier—one of the fast numbers—and I saw Maggie grinding up against Dennis. And then I saw Greg, standing a step inside the door, staring at Maggie through the blood in his eyes.

3

From down the block, I couldn't tell what was what. But as I drew closer, I recognized Maggie's clothes, shredded and strewn over everything. On the lawn, blouses and pants were spread out like suicides that had leapt from the roof. In the street, a leopard skin dress was twisted at the waist and its arms were flailed out to the sides like the victim of a hit-and-run.

I pulled a pair of sliced up pink jeans off the hedges just before I went inside. In the living room, I found Maggie sitting in the chaise lounge, nearly motionless, tightly wrapped in a dingy white robe and wearing large black sunglasses like an insect emerging from a cocoon.

Scattered over the couch and table, I saw her collection of Barbies, which had been brutalized. Blonde heads were disembodied; skinny arms and legs were dislocated.

I laid the pink jeans over a pile of doll parts before finding a seat on the couch. Next to me, a spring jutted out of the cushion and a Barbie head rested against it with its eyes staring up at me. I turned it face down.

In the middle of the floor, the TV remained. A crashed spaceship on a laminate planet. Next to it, sitting atop an overturned cardboard box, a small black & white TV played a picture that blurred around the edges. I watched it, seeing an image of aged, yet delicate hands caressing the forehead and temples of a feeble old woman. The sound was turned all the way down.

"You know what I'm starting to think about this old hangdog?" Maggie said. Her voice was ragged, but steady.

"What's that?"

"I'm starting to think I've actually met him."

"You're crazy."

"No, I'm serious and sane too, and I actually think we've both met him," Maggie said, and while she talked, she remained perfectly still in her cocoon; only her mouth moved. "You remember that church we went to a couple times when we were kids?"

"The one in that strip mall in the ghetto?"

"Yeah, the one that was in that old Super Duper."

"I thought it was in an old wig store."

"No, it was next to an old wig store, but it was in a Super Duper. Remember?"

"No, I can hardly remember it at all. I mean, I was probably only five or six at the time."

"Well, do you at least remember what it was called?" I shook my head that I didn't. "Well, wait until I tell you," Maggie said. "It's going to kill you. It was called the So Help Me God Church of Christ. It said so on a handwritten cardboard sign that was stuck up in the window. And do you remember that inside the church there were just a bunch of old folding chairs and some purple wooden benches?"

"I don't remember any of that. I just remember it being really dim in there and smelling funny. Kind of like mold."

"Right, there were like no lights. Just the light coming in the through the windows, and it smelled terrible. Like medicine. And do you remember the birds? You have to remember the birds!"

"Not at all."

"You don't remember the birds!" Maggie said, and finally broke her stillness, lunging forward at the waist. "How can you not remember them?"

"I just don't. I was too little."

"You don't remember that they were everywhere? All over the sidewalk out front? Sparrows, pigeons, even some crows. All laid out dead from slamming into the window. And I mean really slamming into it. Bam! Like someone slapping their hand against the glass. I can't believe you don't remember that! They slammed into it during the whole sermon. It was like we were under fire. Bam! Bam! Bam! But then, when you saw them laying out front, they looked totally fine. Almost peaceful. I can't believe you don't remember that. They were like the birds in those glass cases at the museum, all neatly arranged in rows with their beady black eyes looking up at you. That's what they were like. Perfect. Completely at peace."

Maggie leaned back in her seat and resumed her cocoon pose, as if to show me how calm the dead birds seemed.

"Why were they doing it?" I said. "I mean, I know it was because they saw their reflection, but why so many right there?"

"I don't know, but that's exactly what I wondered too. And that's how I met the old hangdog."

Maggie gestured toward the TV, and we both watched while they showed a close-up of the hangdog looking heavenward and smiling beatifically. "He was much younger then, of course," Maggie said, "but I know it was him. His skin wasn't as wrinkly as it is now, but he already had his hangdog jowls. And his hands! You should have seen his hands! The fingernails were immaculate. I mean, perfect, like the fingernails of an angel. All buffed and shiny and coming to perfect little points. I noticed them right away, because it was after we came out of the church, and there he was, picking up the birds with his bare hands and putting them into a garbage bag."

"That's nasty," I said. "Did he work for the church or something?"

"He must have," she said, "but who knows? All I know is that even then he had an air about him. Even though he was cleaning up dead birds with his bare hands, he already had it, like he was royalty or something. And I remember I was very intimidated by him, but I still managed to ask what I wanted to ask, which was why the birds did it. And I remember him mumbling something about the window being extra-reflective or something like that. And then I said, 'But isn't there something they can do about it?' And I remember he gave me a real annoyed look. He shot it at me…he literally shot it…and he said, 'Listen, little girl, did you ever try to reason with a bird?' And he said it real hostile-like, and then that was it; he just glared at me, and mom kind of moved me along. And I think that was the last time we ever went there. But that's him! I'd swear to it in court! I'd swear to it on a stack of Bibles! Now that I've remembered those birds, I'd know that hangdog anywhere!"

I was nodding and half-looking at her and half-looking at the TV. "That's pretty amazing, Maggie," I said as I got up and headed toward the kitchen. But she could tell by my tone that I still had my doubts, so she yelled, "It's true, Davey! It's all true!" And then a moment later, when she heard me rummaging around, she yelled for me to fix her one too.

I looked in the pantry for something to eat, but found only three slim jims, a can of beets, a box of cereal and a surplus of canned cat food. Instead, I grabbed a couple beers from the fridge and poured us each a tall whiskey on the rocks.

I headed back in and handed Maggie her drink, and she took it, but did not look up. "For once," she said, "I would like to be the one who leaves. I'm always the one who should, but they always beat me to it."

"Sometimes in spectacular fashion," I said, gesturing around at the destruction.

Lifting the booze, Maggie let it pass between her barely parted lips, and I found a seat back on the couch.

"But you know what the worst part is?" she said.

I glanced around at the destruction again. "What's the worst part?" I said.

"The worst part is that he didn't even believe in dinosaurs."

For a second, I looked up at the ceiling and let her words sink in. Then I looked back at her, squinting. "I have to say, I'm a little surprised that that's the worst part."

"I know, but think about it, Davey—this is the man I've spent the last six years with, and just the other day he decides to tell me that he's pretty sure dinosaurs weren't real."

"Not real, as in he doesn't think they ever existed at all?"

"Yeah, not at all." Her eyebrows rose in two arcs above her sunglasses.

"Does he think all those bones were fake?"

"He said some of them probably were, but mostly he just suspected scientists of making whatever they wanted out of them."

"It's as easy as that, huh?"

"In his mind, it is."

"I suppose that's true."

I picked up the Barbie head that was next to me, turned it over and peered into its vacant eyes. Then, with a soft underhanded toss, I released it into the air. A second later, it bounced off the side of the dead TV, and when I heard the plastic sound that it made, it set off some sort of a spark inside me. For an instant, a vivid memory of the So Help God Church of Christ flashed across my mind. I could picture it perfectly. I could even smell it, like the smell was up inside my nostrils, and I could see all of the birds, a pile of them like a mass grave.

Surely, I thought, the church was gone by now, but the building might still be there, and to this day, birds might still be colliding with it over and over. And with no one there to collect them, there must be an immense pile of them spread over the ground. Not a scattering of them, like the doll parts around Maggie's living room, but a tower of them. A tower of corpses. A warning sign, unheeded by birds that continue to fly over them, rushing blindly to their dooms.

Hospital

I stood next to a stack of dirty bedpans that reached from the floor to the ceiling. At the workstation, two nurses played spades, while three others stood around an emaciated cat, watching it eat greedily from a rusty tin can on the counter. One of the nurses was the one who was training me. A scarecrow of a woman with vinegar in her eyes and a cig pinched between her bloodless lips.

I was tired to the bone. It had been a long time since I had worked in any capacity, and never before as a hospital orderly. I closed my aching eyes for a moment and listened to the sounds of the wee hours: the phlegmy voices of nicotine nurses...the buzz, blip and hum of a million machines...the mirthless rumble of television laughter...patients coughing...their exhausted souls fluttering weakly inside their bodies like moths inside airless jars...

My eyes snapped open as the nurse jabbed me in the ribs with her finger. "Two more patients, hon," she said, "and then we'll call it a night." Her breath hung before me like lighter fluid and cabbage. I followed obediently, head down, yawning.

I stood in the corner of the patient's room, listening to his snores gurgle and pop in his throat. I held a bedpan close to my heart. With the same emotionless whirl as a spider spinning a web, the nurse scurried around the room performing her duties. When her hand, like a withered paw, beckoned, I ceded my bedpan and accepted a dirty one in return. I didn't mind. I just didn't.

The patient was masked. A rubbery affair. Nixon. It still struck me as odd even though I had seen them all night long. Earlier, the nurse had explained: "We had a little problem awhile back with nurses abusing patients. There were beatings and other unsavory-type incidents. To fix the problem, the administration made all the patients start wearing masks. Lots of Nixons and Reagans and some celebrities, too, like Loni Anderson and Tom Selleck. Of course, the nurses still knew the patients weren't who they were dressed up to be, but they couldn't help but treat them better anyway."

"So, it works?" I said.

"The proof's in the puddin'," she said. "Complaints are down forty-eight percent."

Some of the masks were rubber and completely covered the patient's head, but others were pictures clipped from magazines and tied to their faces with string or yarn. A lot of the celebrity ones were like that. And throughout the night, I found myself thinking that's what I'd want—a paper one with string—if I ever wound up in here. Rubber ones are too hot; they make your hair sweat. That is, if you've got any. Lots of them didn't. Most, in fact.

The nurse and I went into a room to check on Princess Di. A paper mask tied on with red ribbon. She had a bounty of long gray hair out the back, which we would have never seen with a rubber mask. It would have been a shame, too, to miss long gray hair. Some people don't like it, but not me. I've always been fond of it, because you can witness in its gray cascade (if you are sensitive to these sort of things) a young girl transforming into an old woman, and an old woman transforming back again.

After the nurse checked the charts, she exchanged bedpans with me. Then she sidled up close to the bed and slid a pen from her pocket. "Listen," she said, and tapped the pen on the patient's knee. "Hear that?" I didn't, but said I did, and the nurse grinned like a chimp. "Metal knees," she said. I nodded, and she tapped the knee a couple more times.

Out in the hall, the nurse lit up another cig and looked at her watch. After a sideways glance, she said, "Come on, we've got a few seconds. Let me show you something we got in last night."

Down a hallway full of flickering brown lights, then down

another and another. Encrusted bedpans lined the walls; rust-bitten stretchers inhabited shadowy corners. Occasionally, I glimpsed the world outside the windows where the sky was slowly turning from black to blue. After riding an elevator with oxidized grilles and creaky wooden doors, we made our way down a hallway that was as dark as an unlit tunnel, and then into a room enveloped in a gelid blue light.

"Know what this is?" she said. And before I could answer, she said, "The morgue."

The nurse swung open a steel door and rolled out a metal slab holding a body covered in a white sheet. I was immensely curious, I must admit.

Slowly, the nurse pulled back the sheet, rolling it in her hands as she did. It revealed a girl—a woman, really—perhaps twenty years old, nude, and covered from head to toe with blue spots about the size of quarters. At first, I thought it was a rare blood disease, and then it crossed my mind that it might be the result of poisoning.

"Know what did it?" the nurse said.

I leaned in closer, seeing that all the spots were sunken in.

"Her husband," the nurse said. "A ball pean hammer. A hundred and sixty-eight times."

My eyes moved slowly over the skin and indentations. "Sad," I said, "but also, in its own way—when one lingers on it, closely—strange and beautiful."

The nurse jerked the sheet back over the body, and I stepped back. She slid the slab back in and closed the door with an echo.

We left.

The Psychic

It was raining and Tim could hear the faint sound of water spraying off cars as they drove by. His brother Dale was eating a cheeseburger and fries, and Tim was eating a fish sandwich and cole slaw. They were in a diner that was down the street from the mill where Dale had worked for twenty-four years, but even from that distance, Tim could smell the smoke, and it seemed he could taste it in his fish.

For the moment, they were silent, but a few minutes earlier Dale had talked non-stop, rehashing his break-up with Arlene. He said Arlene had been perfect for him—he said he would have married her in a heartbeat—but after two years, she had suddenly left him. She told him she wasn't in love with him and didn't know if she was even capable of love anymore. She told him it was her, not him. She said she didn't think she could ever be happy, not even if she had all the anti-depressants in the world. And Dale agreed with her. Yet, four months later, he wasn't over her. He said he was—he said it repeatedly as he told Tim about their break-up—but he wasn't.

Tim dunked the edge of his sandwich into his tarter sauce. Dale asked the waitress for a refill on his Coke, and when she brought it back, he joked with her and touched her arm. He then picked up his cheeseburger with both hands and squeezed the bun as he took a bite.

"I know you don't go in for a bunch of mumbo jumbo," Dale said as he chewed, "but I got to tell you about this psychic I went to a few months ago."

"You went to a psychic?" Tim said.

"Yeah, up in Rayland. Past the titty bars and that ice cream place where the retarded girl works."

He stared at Tim, and Tim looked down and stirred his cole slaw with his fork. Tim was sure he could tell he was embarrassed for him, but it wasn't because he didn't believe in psychics—he didn't know whether he did or not—it was because it seemed to him that someone as broke as Dale should have been saving his money, not spending it on a psychic; but since he had just gone on about his break-up, Tim didn't see any sense in bringing up money too.

"How'd you find out about this psychic?" Tim asked.

"From Kenny Walker down at the bowling alley and his old man," he said. "They both got lucky numbers from her, and both of them numbers hit the Pick 3 within a month. Actually, Kenny hit it twice."

"Did she give you some numbers too?"

"Yeah."

"Did you win anything?"

"Nothing yet, but it ain't been but a couple months."

Tim took a bite of his sandwich and laid the rest on the plate. He sipped his Coke and waited.

"I know you don't believe in hocus pocus like that," Dale said as he chewed another bite of cheeseburger. "But I mean, I was real skeptical too, but when you call to make an appointment with her, you get this answering service, and they don't ask your name or nothing. They just give you a time slot and you show up."

"You show up where?" Tim asked. "At her house?"

"No, it's in some motel," Dale said. "Her husband and her owns this motel that's across the street from their house."

Tim glanced over Dale's shoulder to see if their waitress was anywhere to be found, but he didn't see her. He looked back at Dale.

"Was there anybody else in the room with you?"

"Not in the motel," Dale said, "but I did see her husband in the yard across the street."

"Yeah?"

"Yeah. He was a big fat fella. Tall, too, like Bluto in *Popeye*."

For a moment, Tim thought about her husband and the motel across the street from their house, and he thought about how weird it would feel to walk in there and start talking to a stranger. Tim would want no part of it, but not his brother—he'd talk to anyone. Tim was sure he went in there and started spilling his guts before she even took his cash.

"So, what did she tell you?" Tim said. "Was she accurate?"

"She was amazing."

"She was?"

"Yeah. As soon as I sat down, she started turning over these cards," he said and started using his hands to show how she turned over cards from a deck. "She flipped over a couple cards and without even looking up at me, she said, 'I bet you didn't know that I was born in West Virginia too.'" Dale shook his head and widened his eyes. "Now you tell me how she knew that. She didn't know my last name, and West Virginia isn't exactly written on my face, is it?" He started pretending to turn over cards again. "She flipped a couple more cards and said, 'I see you're forty-four years old.' Then she laid down a couple more and said, 'I see you've been divorced twice, and I see you just got out of another serious relationship.' And she just kept going like that. Everything she said was dead-on the money."

"Everything?" Tim said.

"Everything."

Tim looked over Dale's shoulder and made eye contact with their waitress after she finished with another table. She came over and gave Tim the check and began clearing their dishes. Dale joked with her, and even complimented her on her wedding ring. While he talked about the ring, he held her hand with his fingers. When he was done, Tim handed her the check and some cash and told her they didn't need any change.

When they got out to the parking lot, they stood between their cars. The rain had let up, but everything was still wet, and down the road Tim saw black smoke from the mill spreading across the overcast sky.

"You know, Tim, I'm headed out to see her again tomorrow," Dale said.

"The psychic?"

"Yep. You ought to go along and keep me company."

Tim nodded. "I might just do that."

"Good. I'll give you a buzz in the morning."

They nodded to each other and got in their cars.

*   *   *

In the morning, Dale drove his truck, and Tim sat in the passenger seat and smoked. He could see the river from the road, and every so often he saw a barge hauling coal or a houseboat drifting downstream, but mostly he just saw the water and the tall, thin trees on the muddy bank.

"I tell you what I'd like for you to ask this psychic," Tim said as he stuck his cigarette out the window.

"What's that?" Dale said.

"I'd like for you to ask her why she isn't rich if she has these powers. I'd like to know why she can give lucky numbers to other people, but she isn't a millionaire herself."

Dale was silent for a second. He stared out the window, concentrating on the road. Then he said, "Maybe that's not what's important to her."

"Bullshit," Tim said with a laugh.

Dale laughed too, but then he said, "Seriously, though, maybe that really isn't what she wants."

"Yeah, maybe," Tim said. But the way he saw it was that if she could be rich, then she would be rich, and it wouldn't necessarily be a matter of greed, but one of convenience. Because if she was rich, then she could do her readings or not do them—whichever she wanted—and she wouldn't need to charge people for them. Then, she could share her gift with the world for free.

Tim flicked his cigarette out and rolled up the window.

"So, if you're not going to ask her about getting rich, what are you going to ask her about?"

"Two things," Dale said as he flipped on his blinker and began to slow down. "I want to know what's going to happen with my house and car notes, because at this point, I'm about two months behind on them." Dale rolled the truck up to a stop sign. To the left of them, just a bit down the road, was a motel on one side of the street and a two-story house on the other side. "The other thing is that I want to know if Arlene was cheating on me. She said she wasn't—she swore up and down to it—but that just don't make sense."

Dale made a left turn. Tim looked at him and he looked at the motel. As they rode toward it, Tim told him that he didn't think Arlene was the cheating type. He said he didn't have any evidence to back it up, but from the few times he'd met her, he just didn't get that feeling from her. At least that's how he saw it, Tim said.

Dale nodded, but he didn't say anything. He made a left turn into the motel's parking lot and coasted into a space.

"I'm fixin' to go ahead and ask her about it anyway," Dale said. "Otherwise, it just doesn't make sense."

*   *   *

After Dale had been gone for a few minutes, Tim got out of the truck and walked around to the back of it. He leaned against the truck and lit a smoke. He couldn't have taken more than two puffs when he saw the psychic's husband come out of the house across the street and get into the driver's seat of a car that was parked in their yard. The husband, as Dale had said, was tall and fat. He had dark hair and a beard, and he was wearing a red flannel shirt and jeans. There were four cars and one pick-up truck parked in their yard and none of them looked drivable. After a few seconds, the husband got out of the car and began walking toward Tim. He was carrying two cans of beer that were still held together by the plastic rings from the six-pack.

When the husband reached Tim, he nodded and smiled. "How you doing?" he said. He stood in front of Tim and laid the beers on the asphalt at his feet. "You here to see the psychic?"

"No, I'm here with my brother," Tim said and nodded toward

the room he had gone into. "He already went in."

Tim dropped his cigarette to the ground and mashed it out with his shoe. He slid another one out of the pack and lit it behind his cupped hand.

The husband watched him and grinned. "I'm her husband, Glenn," he said.

"I'm Tim and my brother's Dale." Tim nodded toward the room where Dale was. "He's been here before, so you might've already met him."

"I don't know," Glenn said and shook his head. "She gets lots of them that come back. I'd say just about all of them come back at least once, and then there are some who've been coming for years."

"She's that good, huh?"

"Well, let me put it this way," he said, and then pointed his thumb at their house. "You know she does hair over at the house, right?"

"No, I didn't know that."

"Yeah, she does that on the side. Mostly friends of hers and whatnot. They come over the house and she does different cuts and perms and stuff for them. They do it in the kitchen, you see, and I'm usually in the living room, and usually it's a Saturday or a Sunday, so I'm having some beers and watching racing or fishing. So, last Sunday, she and a bunch of her girlfriends were in the kitchen, and I was in the living room, tossing back a few and watching the race, when all of a sudden there's a knock at the door. So, I get up and open it, and it's one of her friends, Suellen, who happens to be a real looker, and is the type that's always touching on you when she sees you. So, she says 'Hi' to me, and when she does it, she gives me this big, long hug. Well, I tell you, as good as it felt, I was looking over my shoulder the whole dang time, because the wife doesn't like that sort of stuff. But she never came around the corner or nothing, so it seemed okay, and then Suellen went in the kitchen, and I heard the wife and all the girls start talking to her just like normal. But then, about five minutes later, after I had already set back down to the race, the wife came into the living room, and got right up in my ear, and goes, 'Why'd that bitch hug you?'"

Glenn raised his eyebrows and held them up like that for a long time. Then he shrugged and grinned.

"So, you really think she used her psychic powers to know that she hugged you?" Tim said.

Glenn smiled again and raised his eyebrows for a few more seconds, but then he couldn't hold back any longer and let out a big, raucous round of laughter. "No, I'm just fucking with you," he said. "She probably just knew that horny bitch wouldn't keep her hands to herself." He cracked up again, and Tim started laughing too. He then bent down and peeled both beers off the plastic rings.

"Beer?" he said.

Before Tim could answer, he handed him one. They cracked them open and took a couple sips. Then Tim finished his cigarette and flicked it toward the road.

"Let me ask you something," Glenn said, and then he stared hard at the room where Dale and the psychic were. "You ever notice that crazy girls give the best head?"

Tim laughed, and Glenn's grin turned into a toothy smile. "No, I hadn't," Tim said, "but now that you mention it, you might just have something there."

Glenn nodded his head up and down with gusto. "If I rank every blow job I've ever been given," he said, "not a single one will be out of order from the craziest on down."

Glenn's smile widened and he took a drink of his beer. Then he asked Tim if he could spare a smoke, and he gave him one and handed him his lighter. Glen lit it and passed the lighter back. Then he took a long drag and exhaled like it was the greatest cigarette in the world.

"The best head I ever got," he said, "was on my twenty-fifth birthday. Me and a bunch of my buddies were getting all gooned up at the club, and after awhile, a group of girls came over and started drinking with us, and as the night went on, one of them started talking with me. So, one thing led to another, and we ended up out in my truck, and in no time at all, she was going to town, giving me this killer blow job, and she went on working it like that for about five minutes. Then, completely out of the blue, she jerked her head up and stared me straight in the eyes. All hysterical-like, she goes,

'What did they say about me? What did those bitches in there tell you?' And she started crying and threw herself against me." Glenn shook his head and took a drag on his cigarette. "It took me a few minutes to get her calmed down and convince her that I didn't know what in the hell she was talking about. And then, about five minutes later, she was at it again—giving me some of the best head that there ever was."

Glenn flashed Tim his big grin, and Tim cracked up laughing. Leaning back his head, Tim drained his beer and then laughed some more.

"You ever see her again?" Tim said as he crushed his beer can and dropped it to the ground.

"Oh yeah," Glen said as he flicked his cigarette toward the road. "I married her two days later."

When his cigarette hit, tiny orange ashes shot up from it. Tim watched the cigarette butt roll for a few feet before it came to a stop. Then he looked down at the crushed can at his feet. He was just about to ask if Glen had any more, but then he heard the door behind him open. He turned around and saw Dale coming out. The room behind him was dim and gray, and he was walking slowly, like he had just woken from a dream. His mouth was open and his face was white. He looked like he wanted to say something, but couldn't, like someone had just punched him in the gut.

It Was That Kind of Night

Phil had been saying something about religion when Mark held up the bottle of vodka and showed us there wasn't much left. He took a swig and passed it to me, telling me to keep passing it until it was gone, but there was more there than he had thought, and we had to pass it around several times before it was empty.

None of us needed that at that point.

The table we were sitting around was in the back room of my friend Jeff's house. It was late, and most of the other people at the party had gone home or passed out. Aside from me, Mark and Phil at the table, there was also Renee, the interior decorator.

When the bottle was empty, Mark made a big show of turning it upside down to show what we had accomplished, and we all let out a half-hearted cheer. Mark then set the empty bottle in the middle of the table and started replenishing everyone's glasses with scotch and ice.

After Mark finished with our drinks, Phil started up again. He was some kind of professor (I have never known what kind), and he was saying that the whole purpose of religion was to give meaning to life, but he wanted to know what the consequences were of a meaning that came from what we wished was true, rather than what was actually true. He said as far back as he could remember, he knew it was all a sham. He said he had seen through it from the very beginning. He said he probably even believed in Santa Claus longer than he believed in God.

Renee touched his shoulder and said, "I hope you're only talking about organized religion. I hope you're not lumping spirituality into that, too."

"Well, the truth of the matter is that I probably would lump it in there," Phil said, "but it really depends on what you mean by it, I suppose."

"What I mean by it," she said, "is something that I have learned on my own about how life works. About why we are here. It is something fact-based, like a science."

"I think we had better clarify that," Phil said. "Is it science, or is it merely something that is like science? There is a difference, you know?"

"Then, I'll say it is science," Renee said, "because it can be done over and over and others can do it too."

"Well, then, I do look forward to hearing this," Phil said, and he let out a little chuckle and looked at me and Mark, raising his eyebrows at each of us. "I think we all do."

I reached for my scotch and settled back in my chair. "Yeah, let's hear it," I said. I could feel my drunkenness settle heavily behind my eyes.

Renee looked at me for a moment, and then at the other two. She was quite a bit younger than the three of us (as was her husband, who had gone to sleep hours earlier), and she had bright, alert eyes and was quick with a smile. She was sitting erectly, almost defiantly, but just before she responded to me, she seemed to almost suppress a nervous giggle, but then she laid both palms down on the table as if to steady herself. "Well," she said, "this is going to sound a little weird if you've never experienced it, but I don't care how it sounds. You're going to think whatever you want to think anyway." She started to reach for her beer, but then noticed her scotch and took a sip of that instead. "For years now, I've had these out of body experiences. And at first, I didn't even know what they were, because they were so subtle and short-lived. It was like my soul would just slip a little ways out of my body and then slip right back in. It was like having vertigo for a moment. But then, a few years back, I had a full-fledged one. I was lying on my bed, and when I got up, I felt weird, and when I looked back, I saw myself still lying there on the bed."

"Whoa," Mark said.

"I know," Renee said. "I was freaking out. I thought I was dead."

"No shit," Mark said. "I would have too." He was nodding and seemed genuinely interested.

"So, I got scared and laid back down," Renee said, "and I went back into my body right away. And that was it for that time, but then the next time it happened, I was braver and I stayed out longer. And I stayed out longer each time after that, so that now I can leave my room and leave my house, and there are no limits. I can fly, I can pass through things. I can go anywhere I want."

"That's crazy," Mark said. "So, what do you do when you're out? What's the point of it all?"

"Yes, Phil said, "I'd like to know that, as well."

I studied Phil for a second, because the truth of the matter was, I didn't really know him or any of these people that well. We had crossed each other's paths over the years as mutual friends of Jeff, but we weren't really friends ourselves in any real sense. And to be honest, whenever I had run across Phil, he had always annoyed me. He had always seemed so full of himself. And tonight was more of the same. He was wearing the requisite tweed jacket, dark shirt and jeans that so many professors think passes for casual, and his hair was a touch too long and had that purposely messy look to it.

"I'm only just now finding that out," Renee was saying. "I did a lot of research and found out there were tons of people doing this, and, really, anyone can. We're all capable. It's just a matter of tapping into this latent potential. But what I've found out is that this all ties into reincarnation. You see, we are not our bodies; we're our souls inhabiting our bodies. But, the good news is that we do get to pick out our new bodies during the period between our lives. And we make our choices based on what we didn't do well in our past lives. We pick the body that will teach us what we most need to be taught in our next life.

"So, coming back to what Phil said about religion giving meaning to our lives, I do agree that it isn't good to just accept what a church tells us to accept, or to accept something just because it has been passed down for thousands of years, but if it is something that you have been able to experience firsthand again and again, and others have been able to verify it, then that is something you can trust. That is something that gives life a meaning that you can know is real."

When Renee finished, she was smiling and looking at Phil.

But he didn't say anything right away; he just looked at her until she looked down and took a sip of her scotch.

Leaning toward her, Phil tilted his head and looked up over his glasses. He was smiling. And when Renee looked up, he raised his beer bottle and tilted it toward her. She let out the nervous giggle that she had suppressed earlier, raised her bottle, and clinked it against his.

"That's exactly the kind of nonsense I was just deriding," Phil said.

Renee giggled again.

*   *   *

"Okay, I'm going to try to make this simple," Phil was saying. He was standing now, and the rest of us were still sitting. "But it's not simple—not by any stretch—but let me start by saying that the thing that makes us human is that we are humane. Our strongest instinct is to perpetuate the species, or more precisely, our own genes, but I'm not trying to get real technical here." He had his scotch in his hand and it was sloshing all around as he talked.

"We sure do appreciate you dumbing it down for us pinheads," I said.

Renee and Mark laughed, but Phil talked right over them. "That's not what I meant at all," he said. "All I meant was that we've all had a lot to drink here—I know I have—so this isn't the time or place for details and specifics, but it's still worth talking about, even on a very high-level. Don't you agree?"

I shrugged. "Rock on," I said.

Phil squinted one eye at me, but then forced a laugh. "Rock on," he said. "That's good. I'll have to remember that. Okay, I'll rock on." He sat his scotch down on the table and wiped the back of his hand on his coat sleeve. "All I'm saying," he said, "is that we have a strong survival instinct and a strong instinct to protect our young. Our connection with them is stronger than any other animal has with their offspring. And because of this…and this is an important point… we have a strong capacity for empathy that extends *even beyond* our own families. And that makes us unique, you see. That makes us human."

Renee reached out and touched his sleeve. Then she said, "And I don't think that conflicts at all with what I was saying. I can totally see that."

"Well," Phil said, "it conflicts inasmuch as it is based on scientific facts, not baseless assumptions heaped on top of baseless assumptions." He paused and gave Renee a mischievous grin.

"Come on, Phil," I said, "that's a little harsh, don't you think?"

"Ah, she can take it," Phil said, and he reached out and playfully pretended to give Renee a punch on the chin.

"I *can* take it," she said. "It's going to take a lot worse than that to scare me off."

"Right," Phil said. "See there, she's tough." He winked at her, and then seemed to lose himself in his thoughts for a second. He started patting his pants pockets, and then put his hands in his coat pockets. "I'm dying for a cigarette," he said. "I'm going to duck out and have one here in a second, but I want to finish what I was saying first."

"Yeah, I wanted to hear what all you had to say," Mark said.

"Right, of course," Phil said. "What I wanted to mention, sort of as an aside before I go on, is that we not only empathize with others because it comes naturally to us, but we also do it because we are intelligent enough to see that helping others ultimately helps ourselves, because we and our offspring have a greater chance of survival in a less dangerous, more predictable world. I think we can all agree with that, right?"

We all more or less nodded at that.

"Right," Phil said. "So, now I'm going to tie this all into religion, okay? I've shown you that there are very real reasons for what motivates us, or in other words, what gives us meaning, and now I'm going to show how religion, although it is a sham, very naturally fits into that, okay? Here's how. Our desire to be liked or respected or included or however you want to put it….that all stems from our earliest survival skills. You see, because if we are accepted, we are safer, and this is where religion comes in. It has to do with this safety in numbers, and it also has to do with what I said a moment ago about a less dangerous, more predictable world. Because religion's greatest appeal is that it is a way to be included in a system that gives a sense of order to a frighteningly unpredictable situation."

Phil paused at that, as if allowing it sink in.

"Yeah," Mark said. "I follow you. That makes sense."

"Doesn't it?" Phil said. "Therefore—and I honestly believe this—Christianity's long-term success probably has a whole hell of a lot more to do with Paul than it does Jesus, because it was Paul who gave it the appearance of being a logical, hermetic system. He's the one that gave it order, right?"

"Yeah," Mark said, "and it's interesting, too, to think, based on what all you've just been saying, that the religions that promise us eternal life appeal to us so much because they comfort us in the face of our greatest fear, which is—"

Phil had been nodding vigorously and couldn't resist cutting him off. "Not fulfilling our biological role in this life," he said with a triumphant smile.

"Right, man," Mark said. "Exactly. That's some deep shit there."

"That is deep, isn't it?" Phil said with a chuckle, and then he started patting his pockets again. He found a cigarette and started to put it in his mouth, but then stopped short and grabbed for his scotch instead. He downed what was left of it and then put the glass on the table. "I'm going to say one more thing, and then I've *got* to have this cigarette. And this is about religion too, but it's not such academic stuff. It's something personal that I just feel like saying. I don't know why; I just do. It's one of those nights, right, Renee?" He winked at her and picked up his beer. "Like Renee here who said what she wanted to say and didn't care what we thought, I just feel like doing that. You know what I mean? You ever just feel that way?"

My tongue felt thick in my mouth and my eyes were hazy. I didn't feel like hearing another word from Phil, but I said, "Preach it, brother."

Phil laughed loudly and wagged a finger at me. "Very funny," he said. "Very funny, given the topic. But, no, this is serious." And he tried to put on a somber face before going on, but he couldn't and started laughing. "It really is," he said, "but, well, I'm a little drunk, so it is hard to tell it properly, but anyway, here goes." He stood up straight and put his left hand on his heart and raised his right hand. "My name is Phil Wyatt and I'm an alcoholic."

"Hi, Phil," I said. "Welcome. This is a safe space. You're not alone."

"It's good to know," he said. "It really is. But I want you to know that it's true--I really am an alcoholic—but it's also not true. I mean, it's true that I have had trouble in the past with alcohol— really bad trouble—but not anymore. I've got it under control. I mean, I let loose every now and then like tonight—I mean, who doesn't?—but this is rare. It really is. But a few years back, this was every night for me, and it pretty much wrecked my life. I lost my wife because of it; I pretty much lost my kids because of it; and I almost lost my job because of it, and it's a really, really great job. So, I just wanted to tell you that, and I just wanted to give you an example--just one, and then I'll shut up--of how this stuff can get a hold of you and just ruin everything…just turn everything to shit." He took a drink of his beer, looked at the bottle for a second and then give a short laugh. "I'm going to be completely, brutally honest here, okay? I used to fuck a lot of my students, okay? I mean, a lot. Like, at least one every semester. And, at first, I had a system. It was full-proof. Not only did the girls not know about each other, but my wife never suspected a thing. But I got lazy. I got sloppy. I was drunk all the time and that will do that to you. So one night, I was having some drinks with one of my students at the bar in an Applebee's of all places. And she wasn't even one of the pretty ones. I mean, there were so many prettier ones before her, but she was just this kind of big-boned, big -faced girl with a square jaw. Kind of mannish even, but she had long, silky black hair and a nice tan. She might have had a little Native American in her, I don't know. But anyway, she was ready and randy, so I had lured her to this Applebee's that I often lured them to, because it was right by a Red Roof Inn that was perfect for slipping over to after they had had a few drinks. And I was just about to do that with this one, when it all came crashing down. Because, you see, my wife and my son, who was eight at the time, and my daughter, who was ten, had been sitting at a table no more than fifteen feet away, but I was too plastered to even notice. And, of course, my wife could see me the whole time. But she didn't make a big scene; she and the kids just walked up to me, and all she said was, 'Don't ever come home again,' and then she walked out. And believe it or not, I didn't go home. I still went through with the Red Roof Inn thing. And the student—slut that she was—still went through with it too. And the next morning, when I did go home, I found that all the locks had been changed, and I haven't set foot in that house since. It was unbelievable. I mean, when did she get them changed? The middle of the night?"

There was a silence while Phil finished his beer. Then he put his cigarette in his mouth, and said, "Applebee's. Pathetic, isn't it?"

There was another silence while we waited for Phil to go outside to smoke, but then Mark spoke up. "I thought you said that was going to tie into religion somehow," he said.

"Oh, Christ, yes, I totally forgot," Phil said and pulled the cigarette from his lips. "All I was going to say is that people are always telling me—you know how people love to give advice—that I should really look into AA. That is, I mean, they used to tell me that before I got things under control on my own. But here's the thing—I know what causes my alcoholism. You know what causes it? Three things: boredom, meaninglessness, and loneliness. But above all, boredom. I just get so fucking bored if I'm not stimulated, be it intellectually or physically. And so the thing with AA is—and this is kind of funny--is that it appeals to me on one level, because it would be something to get lost in…something to stave off boredom…the way people get lost in religion. That appeals to me. It really does. But the truth of the matter is that it wouldn't last long, because I know it's all a sham. The whole higher power thing. Come on, who are we kidding here?"

Renee spoke up. "I don't think that necessarily has to be God," she said.

"Sure," Phil said, "that's what they say, but come on, we all know what a higher power is. But, hey, don't worry about me, because here's how I see it. The way I see it is that even if I fall off the wagon again, what does it matter? There's no one else I can hurt—they're all gone—and from a biological perspective…from an evolutionary perspective…I no longer serve a purpose. I've already passed on my genes. I've already fulfilled my purpose."

Phil shoved the cigarette back between his lips and gave us a thin grin. "Now let me go smoke this fucking cigarette," he said.

*　　*　　*

Phil went outside to smoke, and Renee went up to bed. And against all better judgment, Mark and I decided to stay up for one more beer. That's when Mark broke out the weed, too.

We passed the pipe back and forth a few times across the table, which was a mess by then. There were crumbs of some sort all over the table cloth, and the empties had multiplied so much that there was hardly anywhere to rest my elbows. Over where Renee had been, there was a spilled drink, but I didn't remember her spilling anything; and the liquid from it was brown and in the shape of Iceland, which I remember amused me when I noticed actual ice cubes slowly melting in the middle of it. In the whole rest of the house, there wasn't a single sound even though there were people sleeping on floors and couches in nearby rooms. And it dawned on me that there had been music playing throughout most of the evening, but someone, at some point, had turned it off. I had no idea when.

Mark tapped out the ashes from his pipe into a glass with a bit of clear liquid in it. He put the pipe in his pocket and yawned.

After a moment, he said, "What about you? You got any Gods in your life? Or demons, maybe?"

"Probably a lot more of the latter," I said.

"But you don't go to church or nothing?" he said.

78

"Well, my wife and daughters do; they hardly ever miss it. So, I go every now and then to make them happy. But it's not like I believe in it or anything. But I don't really mind going for them. I figure, you can still get something out of it even if you don't believe. But it's just so boring a lot of the time, though."

"I feel you," Mark said.

"What about you?" I said. "You strike me as the snake-handling type. Is that accurate?"

Mark made a hissing sound and flickered his tongue, and we both laughed.

"No, really," he said, "it's like this, dude. I'm not anything, but sometimes I'm everything. You know what I mean?"

I smiled and shook my head. "All I know about that statement," I said, "is that you sound like someone who's as high as a motherfucker."

"I am, dude," he said with a laugh, "I am. But I still know what I'm getting at, and that's this: sometimes the only thing that keeps me from being an out-and-out atheist is that I can't completely rule out the possibility of there being a God. So, you see, I don't believe in one, but I can't entirely say it's impossible."

"That makes sense," I said. "You're just being real about it."

"Right," he said. "But other times, dude, even though I intellectually don't believe, I do believe on some kind of emotional or artistic level. You see what I'm saying?

"Not really, but I'm pretty fucking high myself, so it's not you."

"No, that's cool," he said, "But I'm just saying that I can switch back and forth from believing and not believing, depending on the situation. Which is cool, right? I mean, whatever gets you through the night, right, dude?"

"Yeah, right on."

"But now check this out," he said, "'cause here's the coup de gras, my brother. It's all about personal choices; it's all about living your own life however the fuck you want to live it, and making connections along the way, man. So, even though I lean toward atheism or agnosticism or whatever you want to call it, I refuse to be labeled, because to do so would be to take a superior stance to all the other possibilities. Because, for me, identifying with a belief will never be more important than getting rid of pride and being able to embrace, even if just for an hour or a day, someone else's beliefs. You feel me?"

"I feel you," I said. "I feel you."

I rubbed my eyes, and took a sip of my beer. I was so tired and high that I could hardly imagine standing up, but I told Mark I had to go take a piss. I don't know why I didn't just saying I was going to bed, because there was no way I was making it back. But he seemed to know anyway. He just said, "Cool," and closed his eyes.

I made my way into the next room, which was the living room, and had there not been moonlight coming in through the windows, there would have been no way I would have made it through without stepping on the head of some poor sleeper. As I passed through, I could hear breathing and even some light snoring, and I saw a couple people huddled together on the floor, and I recognized Renee's husband face down on the couch. Through the windows, I could see moonlight reflected in patches of slick black mud in Jeff's backyard, and I saw the silhouette of his kids' swing set.

From there, I made my way into a dim hallway. The light there was pale brown, but got darker as I moved down it, until it was black at the end. In the darkness, I turned and started moving my hand in search of the doorknob, and as soon as I found it, I started to turn it. In retrospect, I swear I heard a sound in that instant—maybe an intake of breath, or the rustle of clothes—but I pushed it opened anyway.

It was pitch black in there, but I immediately knew what was what. "Oh, sorry," I said "my fault."

I backed out and closed the door. But before it was completely shut, I heard Phil in the darkness say, "No problem." And after it was shut and I had started to turn away, I heard Renee, in a muffled whisper, say, "Shit."

See a Pretty Thing

When I get to the bar at Dee's, the first thing I hear—I shit you not, the very first thing—is a guy going, "Burt Reynolds never meant shit to me until I discovered his head on a shelf in a laboratory." I already have my scotch and beer, but there's nothing that'll keep me from lingering to hear this.

"But Burt ain't even dead," goes the guy next to him.

"That's what I thought, too," the first guy says. "In fact, I swear to you that was the very first thing that crossed my mind when I realized whose head it was."

"But how could you know for sure?"

"Oh, trust me, I left nothing to doubt. I got right up close to it and run my flashlight over it. It was wrapped in that thick plastic, but I was still able to make out the mustache and that ornery-ass smile of his. Oh, it was Burt all right. No doubt about it."

"But how can that be?" goes the other guy. "I seen Burt no more than two weeks ago on the TV, and it wasn't no old footage neither."

"I'm just telling you what I seen," the first guy says. "You'll have to draw your own conclusions from there, amigo."

After a few drinks, I notice a white man with a white beard going around asking anyone who will listen to name a word he doesn't know. He's quite drunk, loud, abrasive. He's wearing this shirt that's too tight and he keeps tugging and pushing at it, trying to get it just right inside the waist of his pants. He's talking to Kelly the bartender now. He's saying, "You know about Xmas, right?"

"You mean Christmas?" she says. She's getting drinks, wiping down the bar, ignoring him.

"Yeah, Xmas. And you know about Ped Xing, right?"

"What?" she says.

White beard puts his pale and freckled forearms on the bar and leans toward her as far he can. "Do you think it's just a coincidence that in one case we replaced Christ with an X, and in the other we replaced the word 'cross' with an X?"

Kelly drops her rag onto the bar and looks at him. "Do you have a point?" she says.

"Well, don't you see? Now Christ on the cross can be reduced to 'X on X.' It's the crucifixion reduced to algebra."

Kelly looks like she wants to dig out his larynx with a rusty spoon.

I make my way outside. It's just becoming light. I can see the yellow glow of a gas station. I can smell fried chicken, fried fish, fried potatoes. In the parking lot, a shirtless white man sits in his white El Camino. He's smoking. His girlfriend is pushing the car to get it to start it. At the edge of the parking lot there's a black woman wearing orange pants. Her shirt is white and hangs down in the back showing a tattoo across her upper back that says "Chocolate City." Her right arm is broken. It's in an orange cast. There's a white and brown dog walking across the street. It drags a rope from its neck. It stops and takes a quick piss on a three-legged plastic reindeer lying on its side in a yard. The El Camino has made two circles around the parking lot without starting, so I go over, but shirtless guy waves me off. "You don't want any help?" I say. "Naw, she's too fat as it is," he says. "Let her push." I shrug, watch the car slowly go by, watch the girl from behind. I can't see her face. Her hair hangs in dirty brown strings all around it. She's wearing a shabby red hoodie, jeans, work boots. She's got a flat ass, but it's not true that she's fat. I turn away and look through the chain link fence topped with barbed wire next to Dee's. On the other side there's a house that someone spray painted on. The large, hastily scrawled red letters say "Dis my mother fuckin house," but it ain't nobody's mother fuckin' house anymore and hasn't been for years. The windows are all black, most are broken. There are fragments of a plastic birdbath in the yard and the skeleton of a bird on the stoop, but I don't believe the two to be connected. I've studied this scene more than once.

I make my way down the street. It's already daylight. No traces of night remain in the sky. A few third-shifters stagger home like me and the occasional crack ghost lingers in a shadowy doorframe, but mostly the streets are dead. I walk past the graffiti on the brick wall that says "Trust Jesus," and below it, "Trust Yourself." I pass the graffiti on the side of the carryout that says "Chipotle Nick Nolte." In the carryout's window there's a framed painting of an Indian with a tear rolling down his cheek. For years, where the painting is, there was a Dracula mask. A cheap rubber Halloween one. Dracula's face was sagging inward, fangs extracted, flesh collapsing into a mushy skull and moldy brain matter. I remember once someone had wedged a cig into its mouth slit. That made me laugh.

I go under the overpass with the "Love ya Goat" graffiti on it. This is where Teesha used to do haircuts. She had something like a Lemonade-stand-type operation going, except instead of drinks she was selling fades, edge-ups, racing stripes, mohawks and faux-hawks. She always had a long line of dudes waiting for her, because she was good, but then one day, without saying a word to anyone, she just didn't show up, and no one ever saw her again. Someone said she got kidnapped by some dudes in a van—snatched right off the sidewalk where her stand was—but then someone else said she left after graduating high school and was now going to Harvard, so it's hard to tell.

On the other side of the overpass I see the stop sign with the pantyhose tied to its pole. There are several knots and they are tied with such tightness and violence that you'd have to have mitts like the Boston Strangler to get it like that. The pantyhose are messed up from being out in the weather so long. Their color has faded and also turned a kind of a dirty pink and yellow in places. They look like a weird intestinal fuck-up, like what killed that little *Poltergeist* girl whose intestines got all twisted around each other.

I cross the street and go down some steps to Brad's. I knock on the door. It has two gold sixes on it and one black one that Brad drew on with a Sharpee. There's no answer, so I open it and find Brad, Jeff and Hurly lying down, weeded up, watching *Peewee's Playhouse*.

"I love this one," I say.

"Naturally," says Brad from a beanbag the color of a gallstone in the middle of the floor.

It's the episode where Randy makes crank calls that Peewee gets in trouble for.

"Randy," I say. "Best puppet ever?"

"Naw," says Jeff from a nest of blankets on the couch. "Charlie McCarthy. You know how I love the classics."

"Fuck that," Hurly says from the loveseat. "It's Achmed the Dead Terrorist, hands-the-fuck-down."

Brad, in a high-pitched Fred Rogers voice, just goes, "Meow meow meow meow meow meow."

On the coffee table there's a blue bong, a rolled up Maiden poster, a pair of men's underwear. On the floor next to it there's a baby shark in a jar, a lacquered alligator head and a broken ceramic Jesus, presumably all from Florida truck stops. Once or twice a year Brad makes the twenty-four hour round trip to a Taco Tico down there because he's in love with a girl who works there, but he's never spoken to her. Not a peep. He claims a bird (which he swears was an albatross) hit his windshield the first time he ever pulled into that Taco Tico. He takes that to be a sign that he must forever suffer in silence before his beloved. Personally, I think he's just too chickenshit to talk to her, but I've never said so. I couldn't do that to my dude Brad.

"You guys wanna know something crazy about ping pong balls?" Brad says.

"You read my mind," I say. I sit down on the backseat of Brad's old Camaro that now sits on the floor to the side of his beanbag. The seatbelts are intact, but I don't feel a need to strap in.

"Well, actually more than one thing," Brad says.

"Even better," I say.

"Hold on," Hurly says. "Wait a minute. How the fuck do you know so much about ping pong balls all of a sudden?"

Brad struggles to get out of the beanbag and stand up. He's

wearing nothing but a brown robe that smells like a used washrag and a giant faux-gold medallion around his neck.

"If you'd listen," he says, "you'd find out."

"Yeah," Jeff says, "put a sock in it, why don't ya, Hurly."

"Thank you, Jeffrey," Brad says, and he kind of straightens the top of his robe like he's all modest or dignified or something. "I learned about ping pong balls from a truck driver who gave me a lift the last time I went to Florida, and here's interesting factoid number one about them, so get out your pencils. According to the truck driver—who, incidentally, looked a whole hell of a lot like Richard Ramirez—all ping pong balls are made at only one place in the entire United States."

"Seriously?" Hurly says.

"Shut the fuck up," Jeff says at almost the same time.

"Yes, seriously," Brad says. "And here's interesting factoid number two: the way they ship ping pong balls is that they shoot them into the back of a truck with this tube that propels them in, so an entire semi-truck is filled with nothing but loose ping pong balls."

"Whoa," Hurly says, and Jeff instantly shoots him a look.

"So, this truck driver I was riding with," Brad says, "this Night Stalker-looking mother fucker says one time he had a truck full of ping pong balls, and the cops stopped him at some weigh station in Arizona. See, they had been having trouble with truckers bringing drugs through there and they were suspicious, because his truck weighed like nothing. But he told them what the deal was, and he showed them all the paperwork that said what he was hauling, but they wouldn't believe it. They thought no way could his truck really have nothing in it but loose ping pong balls. So, they told him he had to open it up, and he said no fucking way—there'd be ping pong balls all over the whole goddamn highway."

"No shit, man," goes Hurly, and before he is even done, Jeff's sock comes flying across the room and lands on his face. Hurly flings it from him like it's a dead tarantula. "Fuck, man, that's gross."

"I warned you," Jeff says.

"No, you didn't."

"Yes, I did."

"No, you didn't."

"So, anyway," Brad says over top of them, "this cop wouldn't let up. He was bound and determined to see what was in that truck. So, finally, the Night Stalker dude walked about a hundred yards away, and said, 'Okay, asshole, do your thing,' and the cop opened up the truck. And just as you'd expect, he was covered—I mean, completely fucking covered—in ping pong balls. The Night Stalker said he couldn't even see the guy for about ten seconds, and ping pong balls fucking spread out over the earth like a plague."

"Oh, shit," goes Hurly, "did that trucker dude film that shit?"

"No, man, he was too pissed," Brad says.

"Aw, man, that shit could have been on America's most funny as fuck videos and shit."

"Indeed," says Jeff, who starts stripping off his other sock.

"So, those are the facts, Jack," Brad says, and spins on his heel and plops back down into his beanbag, but before the whoosh of air has even finished leaving the beanbag, Hurly has staggered to his feet.

"Listen, dudes," he says as he makes his way front and center, "I wanna talk about my plan."

"Aw, Christ," goes Jeff.

"No, I know you guys have all heard it, but he hasn't," Hurly says and points at me. "I think he'd be down with it."

"He's not going to be down with it," goes Brad.

"Well, you never know," goes Hurly.

"Sometimes you do," goes Jeff.

"Listen, man," Hurly says and looks at me, "I've got this idea for robbing the A-rabs that run the corner store."

"You mean the Indians?" I say.

"Yeah, that's what I said—the A-rabs."

I just let it go, because Hurly is what you would call a real, live fool. I mean, just look at him: a scrawny, skeletal white dude with the dirtiest dreadlocks you've ever seen, a receding hairline, a Venom *Welcome to Hell* t-shirt and some battered as hell snakeskin boots.

"I need three people to do the job," he says, "but neither of these twinkies here want in. But Lesbo Annie's gonna do it, so I just need one more, which is where you come in, my brother."

"So what's the idea?" I say.

"Simple. Lesbo Annie, see, while she's buying something at the counter, falls to the floor and fakes a seizure to distract the cashier, while you and I fill our pockets with anything that ain't nailed down."

Jeff gives a snort, and Hurly gives him a hard stare.

"First of all," I say, "that's shoplifting, not robbery."

"Yeah, but we'd still get some serious loot," he says. "Those A-rabs got all kids of shit in that place."

"And second of all—"

"Second of all is he ain't gonna do it," Jeff says.

Hurly glares at him. "Will you just let him talk?" He looks at me hopefully. "And second of all?"

I get up, look in his eyes to see if he's for real—to see if there is even anyone awake at the wheel in there—and then I give him a pat on the back.

"Second of all is I'm not going do it," I say. I make my way to the door to the sound of laughter from Jeff and Brad.

"Laugh now," I hear Hurly saying as I head out, "but you guys just wait..."

I make my way back up to street level and past the front yard with the three gazing balls and a cement pig. There's a naked Barbie in the yard, and a battered orange cat on the porch giving me the evil eye. On the sidewalk, I step over a burrito with a single bite out of it. A few feet later I step over an empty dildo box and a dingy pair of women's panties, and I can only imagine the sequence of events.

I cut down the ally with the "Hard Times" graffiti. In an area overgrown with weeds, over by a chain link fence, there are hundreds, if not thousands, of empty 40s—King Cobra, Colt 45, Schlitz, Magnum, Olde E, the whole gamut. I call it the 40 graveyard. It has been growing for years, but I almost never see anyone there, but this morning there is actually a crack ghost in a *Flashdance* shirt picking through the rubble. She's oblivious to me. She is wearing some type of stretch pants, and her shriveled ass and withered legs look inhuman. I think of a praying mantis and half-expect her to come up from the 40s feeding on a grasshopper clenched tightly in her forelimbs, bug goo dripping from her chin.

I reach Lesbo Annie's backyard, and wave to her and Jeni sitting on a couch on her back porch. For breakfast they're having screwdrivers and cigarettes. I make my way past the pink flamingoes and a headless, naked, male mannequin sitting on a toilet. On the porch, I lay down on the long folding beach chair next to the couch.

"What're you up to this beautiful morning?" Lesbo Annie says.

"Well, I hit Dee's after work," I say, "and then went and saw the dudes for a minute, and now I'll probably head home and catch some Zs before heading back over to Dee's."

"You're off tonight then?"

"Yes, thank God."

The sun is blazing over their shoulders and I shade my eyes as I look at them. Lesbo Annie's drab brown hair looks like she cut it herself again, and she has several red pimples around her nose and one amazingly yellow, pulsating one right at the corner of her mouth.

"What are the dudes up to?" Jeni says.

"Same old same old," I say. "Except Hurly's plotting a robbery, that's all."

Jeni rolls her eyes. She has a big meaty face and a massive head of bleached blond hair that hangs off her like hay.

"We heard," she says.

"Yeah, and I hear Annie's in on it," I say.

"Yeah, right," Lesbo Annie says with a snort, and the two of them cackle like a couple of magpies. Then Lesbo Annie puts her Virginia Slim into the corner of her mouth right next to the pimple and takes a long-ass drag.

"That dumb mother humper couldn't—" Lesbo Annie starts to say, but then we all hear a bell like you might hear on a little girl's bicycle, and we all look up and wave at Larry going by on his bike.

"Little hellion," Lesbo Annie mumbles.

"Yeah," Jeni goes, "did Annie tell you he's planning a school shooting?"

"Larry?" I go.

"Yeah, Larry. Tell him, Annie."

Lesbo Annie shrugs and crushes out her cigarette in an overflowing ashtray lying at her feet.

"He's for real about it," she says. "He showed me the plans he has, told me about all the weapons he's amassed, showed me the hit list he's worked up. Lot of thought's gone into it. It's impressive."

"Are you serious?" I say. "What's he in, like middle school or something?"

"Yeah, something."

"Well, don't you think you should say something to somebody?"

Lesbo Annie cocks an eyebrow, makes a scoffing sound and looks at Jeni and then back at me. "He ain't got the guts," she says.

"But how do you know?" I say.

"I just do."

"But how?"

"Listen, that boy couldn't pour piss out of a boot if the instructions were written on the heel. Ain't that true, Jeni? Tell him what Larry asked you the other day."

"You mean about us being lovers?" Jeni says.

"Yeah," Lesbo Annie says. "Now listen, this is true."

A smile crosses Jeni's big meaty face and she goes, "He asked me the other day if me and Annie here are lovers, right? And I said to him, 'Well, I don't believe in love, but if what you mean is do we fuck, then, yeah, we fuck.' Well, you could have picked up his jaw at that."

Lesbo Annie starts cackling like mad and goes "Tell him the rest."

"I'm fixin' to, you crazy bitch." Jeni shakes her head and laughs. "So, then he goes, 'How's that possible, you don't have dicks, do you?' And it dawns on me that this little cretin who thinks he's gonna blow up a school doesn't even know what lesbian sex is."

"Or that you can fuck without a dick," says Lesbo Annie with a phlegmy laugh.

"Or with a big old rubber dick," goes Jeni, and they both lean into each other and yuk it up. "So, I learned him on the gay birds and bees. Pussy eating, dildo fucking, rim jobs, the whole nine yards."

"Makes you wonder what they're teaching in them schools, though, don't it?" Lesbo Annie says. Then she checks her drink, nudges me and asks if I want one.

"Yeah," I say with a yawn. "Or maybe not. Or I dunno, maybe." I lie back and close my eyes. "You ladies don't mind if I just crash right here, do you?"

"Look at you," Lesbo Annie says as she makes for the door. "Tired as a whore on nickel night. You just go ahead and do what you need to do, baby, and Annie'll fix you up a little drink just in case."

Lesbo Annie goes in and I hear the screen door slam a few times behind her.

When I wake up, she and Jeni are gone and there's a warm screwdriver on the porch beside me. It's dark out. I hear a distant siren and someone's dog going nuts. I take a gulp of the screwdriver and toss the rest off the porch. Then I head over to Dee's.

When I get there, the first thing I hear—I shit you not, the very first thing—is a guy at the bar going, "How do you think you would have held up in a concentration camp?" I already have my scotch and beer, but there's nothing that'll keep me from lingering to hear this.

"I'd have been fine," goes the guy next to him. "No problem."

"How the hell do you figure?"

"Because I've got something most other people don't have."

"What's that, besides a bunch of bullshit?"

"I've got no fear of death."

"Oh, come on," goes the first guy, "that's not even possible. Besides, the real question is do you think you would have actually survived a concentration camp?"

"Probably."

"You do realize that only one out of every twenty-eight prisoners survived in the camps?"

"I did not know that," goes the other guy, "but outside of the camps, zero in every twenty-eight are surviving, so I'll take my chances on the inside."

After a few drinks, I notice a chubby guy with a red beard. His fly is halfway down and his fingers look like Vienna sausages. He's talking to Kelly the bartender, and he's saying, "Pretty girl like you, you ought to think about getting your teeth whitened."

"How about I just get them all pulled instead?" she says. She's getting drinks, wiping down the bar, ignoring him.

"Joke if you want to," goes red beard, "but I'm being serious here. You'd look like a goddamned model if you got some whitening done."

Kelly drops her rag onto the bar and looks at him. "How about I just start out with lightening them instead?" she says. "I don't want to jump right into whitening, because you know how it's so distracting to talk to someone whose teeth are too white. It's like a chick whose tits are too big. You know what I mean?"

"Well, I don't even know if lightening is a real thing," red beard stammers.

"Well, I think I've heard of it."

"Really? Where?"

"You know, commercials, the newspaper, almanacs."

"Almanacs?"

"Maybe. I don't know."

Kelly barely gets her last word out before things in Dee's take a sudden turn for the twilight zone. She sees it at the same time I see it: a man with pantyhose over his face walks through the door. Instantly, he starts waving a gun around and yelling. I can't make out a word of it, but people panic—they duck, scatter, yell and scream—and I feel panic seize me too and everything shrinks down to tunnel vision. My skin is tingling and I feel like I might pass out. I literally feel my legs start to tremble. But then I notice a few things: first, I notice that the man waving the gun and yelling his head off has dirty white-boy dreads sticking out the back of the pantyhose, and then I notice he is wearing a Venom *Welcome to Hell* t-shirt, and finally I notice his snakeskin boots look more like they were made from the flesh of a sun-scorched earthworm than any snake. Suddenly, I feel just fine.

Amid the panic, I catch sight of Lesbo Annie and Jeni over in the corner by the dartboards and I can see they've recognized Hurly too; and Lesbo Annie falls to the floor and starts seizuring, and then Jeni falls alongside her and seizures too, until the too of them are half-seizuring and half-cackling like mad.

"Christ, Hurly," I say as I walk toward him.

He sees me coming and points the gun at me. Right at my chest.

"Back the fuck up, dude!" he yells like he doesn't know me. "I'm warning you!"

"Hurly," I say as I get right up on him and push the gun out of the way, "put a sock in it, will you."

I walk past him and out the door. I can still hear the sounds of panic behind me for a moment, and then the door shuts and I don't hear it anymore.

I cross the street and walk past the graffiti on the side of the liquor store that says "Loco Sam Loves All Ladies," and I know in my heart that he does. There is a smashed Styrofoam cup on the ground and a half-empty bag of Funyuns. I can smell the sewer, fried fish, fried chicken. There are cars cruising up and down the street and lots of people. Some walking, some standing on corners and outside stores, some sitting on stoops and porches. It is dark out. I stop and look up. There's not a single star to be seen anywhere in the sky. There never is around here. It's always just a haze of black.

Cool Jerks

1

Bundy popped some speed and swallowed it with his last drink of beer. Keeping one hand on the wheel, he crushed the empty can and dropped it behind the passenger seat. He then pulled a new one from a crumpled brown bag at his side. On the other side of the bag, sitting in the passenger seat, Mike slowly sipped a beer of his own. He was slouched in his seat and his sunglasses were riding low on his nose. His drowsy eyes scanned the city's darkening skyline as he and Bundy made yet another loop around the city's outer belt. Aside from stopping to take an occasional piss and get gas, they had been circling the city for nearly twelve hours. They had vowed to do so—no matter how long it took—until the radio played "Cool Jerk", a song they had once heard in shop class when Mr. Cruise had let them listen to the radio.

With his right foot propped up on the dashboard and his beer in his right hand, Mike used his left hand to press the Seek button on the radio. Each time the tuner stopped on a station, he announced either the group or genre: "Aerosmith...Mary J. Blige...Christian Rock... Religious Talk...Classical..."

Bundy lit a cigarette and took a few long drags.

"...Country ...Bryan Adams... Heavy Metal... Echo and the Bunnymen ...Smooth Jazz ...commercial..."

"Hey, man," Bundy interrupted and pointed his cigarette toward Mike's shoe on the dashboard. "You know what you ought to get?"

"What?"

"Those kind of leather shoes that have square toes and a zipper up the side. They're like a 3/4 cut and you zip them."

"Yo, man, those are tight!" Mike said and momentarily stopped changing the radio stations. "That one guidance counselor in high school used to rock those all the time."

"I think I had a teacher who wore those too."

"Yeah, but Mr. Grinston had it going on," Mike said and fired up a smoke for himself. "You remember him? He wore these tight, dookie green pants that he tucked into the shoes. And he had a gray Jheri curl that was, like, dry."

"I can't remember him, but let me guess—he had a goatee too," Bundy said.

"Yeah, right," Mike said. "And he wore a tight, leather, Members Only jacket."

"What color?"

"Gray."

Mike and Bundy both cracked up.

"Man, I wish you could remember him," Mike said as he leaned toward the radio but stopped short of pressing the Seek button. "He wore these rings that were somehow too small and he had these long, pimped-out fingernails. And he was always sporting, like, three gold chains…like, one 16 inch, one 18 inch and one 22 inch."

"He took it to that level, huh?" Bundy said.

"Yeah, he was serious about it."

Mike pressed the Seek button and took a sip of his beer. It was nearly dark out, and the skyline—partially lit up and partially draped in darkness—looked placid, as if uninhabited. The traffic on the outer belt, which had been heavy for the last few hours, had now begun to thin out; the remaining cars seemed to shoot past like jets.

"…The Cars, I think …Amy Grant …Tool …commercial …commercial …Usher…"

Bundy crushed his cigarette into the ashtray and immediately lit another one.

"Was he helpful?"

"Huh?"

"Mr. Grinston," Bundy said. "Was he a helpful guidance counselor?"

"Naw, man, he was terrible," Mike said. "Like, if you asked him, 'What do you think I should do?' he'd shoot back, real hostile-like, 'Well, what do *you* think you should do?' and then he'd just stare at you until you got up and left."

2

It was 3 A.M., and Bundy and Mike had finally given up their quest for "Cool Jerk." Bundy was standing in a dark parking lot. There were several other people standing in the parking lot too; they were all talking and laughing and, like Bundy, waiting for food.

Mike, who had stayed behind to talk to someone inside the rib joint, came out and made his way over to Bundy, where he stopped and took a long drink from his can of beer.

"You leave yours in the car?" Mike asked.

"Yeah," Bundy said. "I'm going to get it in a second. I was just waiting to see how long the line was."

Mike nodded and took another drink of his beer.

The cars in the parking lot were parked haphazardly and a few of them had turned on their headlights, creating an asymmetrical web of light. One of the cars was booming out some Nas, and another kept honking its horn every few seconds. Periodically, a thin young black girl would stick her head out of the rib joint's door and holler out a name.

"Who was that guy you talked to back in there?" Bundy asked as he lit a cigarette behind his cupped hand.

"You didn't recognize him?"

"Huh uh."

"Man, that's that dude that tried to kiss Abe at that one party we went to."

"Oh shit," Bundy said as he laughed smoke out of his mouth. "I recognize him now."

"Yeah, that's him."

Mike partially sat down on a large trashcan that was at his side. With a cigarette dangling from his lips, he nodded his head to the music.

"You ever hear what happened at that party after we left?" Mike said without removing the cigarette from his lips.

"The one where that guy tried to kiss Abe?"

"Yeah."

"Huh uh, what?"

"Well, you remember that guy who tried to kiss Abe was there with his sister, right?"

"Yeah, I remember because he and his sister were grinding to the music like they wanted to fuck each other, while his sister's boyfriend just stood off to the side looking like a chump."

"Yeah, yeah, right," Mike said enthusiastically. "Well, sometime after we left, the sister ended up stabbing her boyfriend with a butcher knife. Once in the back and once in the side. They had to rush his ass to the emergency room."

"Did he die?"

"Naw, but I guess he was pretty fucked up."

"Yeah, no shit," Bundy said and flicked his cigarette into the darkness. "So, did she go to jail or whatever?"

"Hell naw," Mike said with a laugh. "They was living together again by that following Monday."

Bundy laughed and shook his head.

"Crazy, ain't it?" Mike said.

"It sure as hell is."

Bundy glanced over his shoulder to see if the girl was sticking her head out of the rib joint's door, but saw only a closed screen door through which a pale yellow light fell onto the dirt outside. Bundy pointed toward the car to indicate that he was going to get his beer. Mike raised his can to let him know that he'd take another.

When Bundy returned, he handed Mike his beer and cracked open his own.

"Guess what?" Bundy said as he placed a cigarette between his lips.

"What?" Mike said.

"When I was in the car getting our beers, I flipped on the radio on a whim, and guess what I heard?"

"No…" Mike said with amazement.

"Yep," Bundy said. "Heard It In A Love Song" by the Marshall Tucker Band."

Mike pursed his lips. "Fuck you."

"What? I thought you liked that song."

"Fuck you."

Bundy laughed and took a long drink of his beer.

3

The car smelled of pot smoke, barbeque and collard greens. Quietly, the radio emitted "I Was Made To Love Her" while Mike and Bundy passed a joint. Through the dirty windshield, they watched the sun rise over a blank, dingy white drive-in movie screen.

"We should try and find Mr. Grinston," Bundy said as he reached for the joint with his barbeque-stained fingers.

"Lloyd?" Mike said as he held in his smoke.

"Huh?"

"Lloyd," Mike repeated, and then exhaled. "His name was Lloyd Grinston."

Bundy, having just taken a hit off the joint, widened his eyes at Mike's remark. Gradually, a smile crept over his lips as he desperately tried to hold in his smoke, but he lost it as soon as Mike started laughing too.

"His fucking name was Lloyd?" Bundy said amidst laughter and coughing. "Who the fuck names someone Lloyd?"

"Yeah, man," Mike said. "Crazy, ain't it?"

"Yeah, it is…yeah, it is…"

Bundy passed the joint back to Mike, and then, still seated in the driver's seat, turned around and started searching the back seat for a beer.

After taking a short hit off the joint, Mike began smoking it like a cigarette. Slowly, his eyes closed into narrow slits and smoke sleepily twirled up from his slightly parted lips.

On the radio, Stevie Wonder segued into The Four Tops' "7 Rooms of Gloom". Outside the windshield, the sun sparkled on every side of the movie screen, surrounding it like an aureole. Behind it, cars zipped by on the interstate; they started on the right-hand side, disappeared behind the aureole, reappeared on the left-hand side, and then abruptly dropped off the edge of the earth as they made their way around a curve.

Coming up empty in his search for a beer, Bundy turned around in his seat and put the car in Drive. He knew of a little carryout down the road apiece, and if it wasn't open, then they could always swing over to Mike's house where they could have a few beers before they crashed.

"Hey, what do you think Grinston would have done if his old lady would have stabbed him a couple times like that broad did to her boyfriend at that party?" Bundy asked as they sped down the road. "You know, like, if Grinston had a little too much to drink one night and she just got fed up with it and stabbed his ass."

"First off, Grinston's old lady would never stab him," Mike said. "If anything, she might throw hot grits or hash on him, but stabbing him would be out of the question."

"But what if he was really drunk...you know, like, sloppy drunk?"

"No way, man," Mike said. "Grinston was a stud. In those tightass pants that he wore, his dick looked like a Pringles can taped to his leg."

"For real?"

"For real," Mike said. "Now, you tell me what kind of broad's going to take a chance on losing that."

With a burned out joint dangling from his lips, Mike put his sunglasses on and allowed them to slide down his nose.

As they neared the carryout, Bundy slowed down, even though it was obvious that the place was closed. Creeping past it, he watched the car's reflection undulate in the dim glass of the store until it disappeared into the edge of the window. Then he sped back up.

"We need to go to your place and crash," Bundy said. "And then you know what we need to do?

"It doesn't involve 'Cool Jerk,' does it?"

"Naw, man, I honestly can't even remember how that song

goes."

"Me neither, dude. But it was cool; I remember that."

They were too tired to give more than a little laugh as Bundy turned onto Mike's street. At the end of the block, they could see Mike's house; it was the one with the couch on the porch and a disco ball that he'd found in the neighbor's trash hanging above it.

"What we should do," Bundy said, "is really, truly try to find Grinston. We should study the dude. See where he hangs, what he drinks, what he eats, the company he keeps."

"I don't think so, bro."

"Why not? It'd be cool as hell."

"'Cause Grinston's dead, dude."

"Dead?"

"Yeah, man, I remember my parents talking about it about a year ago. They said his landlady found him out on his patio, sitting in a lawn chair, wearing nothing but his smoking jacket and flip flops. Cold as an ice cube, they said. He must have been out there all night."

Bundy slowed down and hung a right into Mike's driveway, sending a couple of mangy stray cats running. "Crazy world, ain't it?' he said as he eased around a busted up shopping cart that took up part of the driveway.

"It sure as shit is," Mike said. "But I wouldn't have it any other way."

Bundy clicked off the ignition. He and Mike glanced at the house, but neither made a move for it. Bundy folded his arms over the wheel and laid his head on them, and Mike slouched deep down in his seat and let his head ease back on his neck.

Before the engine's last ping, both were out like a light.

Squeaky Device

1

On Christmas morning in Alderson, West Virginia, as the few visible white stars in the sky transformed into gray snowflakes meandering toward the ground, Penny sat inside her trailer, watching static on a small black and white TV. From within the crackling and flickering snow on the television screen, bits of a news story sporadically seeped out: "...for Christians worldwide...the birth of Jesus...this date also...in Alderson, West Virginia...a significant anniversary...ten years since...the device...in the center of town... discovered...near the prison...a leather strap...a rusty nail...a rustic wooden post..."

For a moment, Penny thought back to when she first heard about the device. About how some boys who were rabbit hunting came across it; about how Alderson was swarming with reporters and cameramen for weeks afterward; about how the device was installed in the center of town, where it remains to this day, surrounded on all sides, at all times, by armed guards. Penny's mind began to swirl with the faces and names of those who had been subjected to it...all the famous cases that had been solved by it and the media attention that accompanied every case. Penny tried to match names with faces and cases with dates, but she couldn't manage it. Recently, her mind had been so fragmented...so fidgety and erratic...like an electrical wire in the final throes of short-circuiting...or like a TV crackling static and spurting out fragmented reports…

"…escaped two days ago…she is still believed to be in the rugged highlands surrounding the prison…officers and police dogs…searching tirelessly…it is believed…ultimately…Squeaky…to California…to reunite with Charles Manson…"

Penny glanced at the clock and then clicked off the TV. Her mom had gone down the hill to pick up Penny's younger brother from their grandparents' house and would be back any minute. As Penny leaned forward, extending her right arm, her lank fingers jittered. The skin on her hairless forearm was yellowish, nearly translucent around her narrow radius, and her fingernails were ragged on the ends and raw around the cuticles. From the plate, she scooped into the palm of her hand scrambled eggs and several tiny pieces of sausage, which she then wadded up inside a paper towel that she tucked inside the pocket of her baggy pink sweat pants.

After putting on her older brother's big winter coat and heavy black rubber boots, she left the trailer and ducked into a small patch of woods out behind it. She often hid her food out there, under a rock or under some leaves, but today she went farther into the woods, until she was on the other side, where they ran alongside the railroad tracks and the abandoned boxcar that had rested there for years.

Unwrapping the paper towel, Penny glanced over her shoulder, and then began flipping pieces of egg toward the big dark square opening on the side of the boxcar. After awhile she stopped tossing the pieces one by one and balled up the remaining food inside the paper towel, which she tossed from her hand and watched through squinting eyes as it arced, then swiftly plummeted into the pitch black opening on the side of the boxcar.

Then Penny turned and began to walk away, but before she entered the woods, she heard a woman's voice behind her.

"Will you help me?" the voice said.

Penny turned around and saw, standing upright, leaning against the edge of the boxcar's opening, a pale, naked woman with long, matted, brown hair. The woman's body was smeared with what appeared to be either dirt or ashes. The only item that she wore was a long necklace that hung all the way to her navel. At her side, the woman was holding an opened book, and as Penny walked toward her, she saw that the pages contained black and white photographs of bones scattered across and partially buried in dry dirt.

"Will you help me?' the woman said again as she backed into the darkness.

"If I can," Penny replied and entered the boxcar, too.

Once inside, Penny was surrounded by the scent of ashes and animal urine. The inside of the boxcar was lit by a single candle. The woman laid the book, opened to the photographs, on a stack of wooden boxes, which the woman stood behind. In the flickering light, Penny glanced at the woman's naked body and was startled to see numerous coarse reddish-brown hairs sprouting from around her nipples, and a thick layer of dried brown blood on her inner thighs; and she could now see that the necklace that hung down to her abdomen was adorned with the skulls and various bones of small animals.

"I was told that I could give birth to a new universe if I became pregnant through intercourse with this corpse," the woman said as she peered down at the opened book. "But now I can't quite figure out how to manage it."

Stepping around to the side of the boxes where the woman stood, Penny could now see the photograph better. The bones were not randomly tossed onto the ground; instead they formed a nearly complete skeleton, and upon some of the bones Penny could see shreds of desiccated flesh and muscle.

"Are you supposed to use that long bone?" Penny asked as she pointed toward a dusty gray femur.

"I suppose so," the woman responded, "but how do I get it off the page?"

Penny fingered the edges of the page and slightly turned the book from side to side searching for an angle from which the page could be entered. As she did so, her wrist and part of her forearm poked out from the sleeve of her jacket.

"So, you are starving yourself?" the woman asked.

Penny looked at the woman, and then looked down at her own forearm. She reached for the edge of her sleeve in order to cover herself, but the woman reached out and touched her hand.

"Leave it," the woman said. "I don't mind."

Gently, the woman embraced Penny from behind and guided her down onto her knees. Once she knelt down alongside the woman, Penny's sleeve was rolled up and her narrow forearm was laid across the book, exactly over the femur in the photograph. Slowly, the woman placed Penny's hand between her naked thighs and softly squeezed them closed around her fingers. Without any perceptible movement from either of them, Penny's fingers, and eventually her entire hand, entered the woman's warm, blood-filled vagina.

They were silent for a long time before the woman, bending down slightly toward Penny, spoke in hushed tones: "When I reentered the world with the intention of creating a new universe, I thought I would be alone, but I'm pleased that I am not."

Penny removed her hand from the woman's vagina and wiped blood from her palm onto the woman's thighs.

The woman found a box to sit on, and Penny found one too.

"Creating a new universe can be a lonely endeavor," the woman said. "I have known from the beginning that my creation will eventually rebel against me and deny me in order to become like gods themselves. This apotheosis of theirs will be an illusion, of course, but the rebellion is inevitable nonetheless."

Penny wrapped her arms around herself to ease her shivering. Outside, the sky was growing lighter, and through the opening on the side of the boxcar, along with the snowflakes, pale yellow light entered and gradually spread itself over the walls.

In silence, the two women drifted off to sleep.

2

At dinner on the day after Christmas, Penny excused herself from the table, leaving behind a plate covered with soggy French fries smothered in gravy, a hamburger torn into several small pieces and peas that had been smashed by the back of her fork. She had gone to take a warm bath, and before getting into the tub she turned on the radio that sat on the back of the toilet.

In the bathtub, only Penny's head, kneecaps and a small portion of her lower thighs were visible. The rest of her body was hidden beneath the motionless gray water. As Penny looked at her wasted thighs and kneecaps, she did not see them as they were, but instead as thick, lumpy slabs of meat. She was ashamed of them, even alone in the bathtub, so she closed her eyes and submerged her legs in the water.

"In Alderson news," a newswoman on the radio reported, "only a day after the 10th anniversary marking the discovery of the town's famed device, it has been removed from the town square by U.S. military personnel. The famed device consists of a long, well-worn, brown leather strap nailed to a rustic wooden post. The leather strap, when wrapped around someone's neck, makes it impossible for the person to tell a lie. Very similar, as many people have pointed out over the years, to the lasso used by fictional super heroine Wonder Woman."

Penny quickly got out of the bathtub, wrapped a towel around herself and began yelling for her mother and brothers to come hear the news. As soon as they heard it was about the device, they all came running, and like all of Alderson, listened in silent disbelief.

"Hours before the U.S. military was deployed into Alderson, local police had discovered escaped convict Lynette 'Squeaky' Fromme in the center of the town with the leather strap from the device wrapped around her neck. It is believed that she discovered the device at some point during the night. How she overtook the security guards remains a mystery. However, it is believed that she didn't work alone. Yet, there was no one else with her when she was discovered, and all of the security guards had been slain by knife wounds to their throats.

"According to a medical examiner, Ms. Fromme had likely been subjected to no less than six hours under the influence of the device. According to experts, since it was impossible for her to lie, she needed only to speak out loud about something in order to give a comprehensive, flawless, truthful explanation of that particular subject. Throughout the night, Ms. Fromme allegedly spoke out loud on numerous subjects, including metaphysics, epistemology, ethics, political theory, language, art, mathematics, science and religion.

When authorities found her this morning, she was gnashing her teeth, pulling her hair from her head, beating her breast and screaming, 'I have seen God!' over and over again. According to police sources, the military had little alternative; Ms. Fromme was swiftly removed from the scene and executed soon thereafter at an undisclosed location somewhere in the hinterlands surrounding the town."